AMIKUK

AMIKUK

by Rutherford G. Montgomery

Illustrated by Marie Nonnast

The World Publishing Company

Cleveland and New York

Library of Congress Catalog Card Number: 55–5278

FIRST EDITION

For Judy Kirks

CONTENTS

LIST OF ILLUSTRATIONS

AUTHOR'S NOTE

The time in this book is a period previous to World War II when the extermination of the sea otter seemed certain. This date was selected in order to present the Aleuts as they lived before extensive changes took place. With the coming of the army and the navy to the islands, the sea otters have received protection which has enabled them to increase in numbers to some extent.

RUTHERFORD G. MONTGOMERY

AMIKUK

1 : STORMY CRADLE

The day was not unusual for the Aleutian Islands, which extend for a thousand miles southwestward from the Alaskan coast. These islands are little more than a chain of submerged mountain peaks rising as a barrier between the Bering Sea and the Pacific Ocean. Here the icy winds off the Siberian coast meet the warmer air from the Japan current in the Pacific, and the weather which this meeting breeds is the worst mixture of rain and sleet and fog and savage winds that can be found any place on earth.

A hurricane gale hurled billows of black fog over a ragged reef, seething currents rushed in and out of passages between the rocks. The roar of the breakers and the wind blotted out the harsh cries of the water birds along the shore. The churning waters off Black Reef seemed an unlikely place for

Bobry clasped Amikuk to her breast as she floated on her back.

any animal, or fish, to make its home. Even a powerful swimmer was likely to be beaten to death upon the rocks or swept out to sea by the savage undertow. But there was a dweller of this bleak scene who made the reef his home. Nor was he a transient who stayed only part of the season, like the gulls and the terns. This was his home, spring, fall, winter, and summer, and he lived there with his mate and his first-born son, who was two weeks old.

Kahlan, the sea otter, was taking a nap amid the confusion of wind and water. He floated on his back, anchored in place by a rope of kelp which he had wrapped around his middle so securely that the currents could not sweep him away. His forepaws were folded upon his chest, and his big webbed hind feet were crossed tightly behind his tail. The sea around him seethed and churned, lifting him high into the air and then dropping him down into the trough of a wave. Neither the noise nor the buffeting disturbed him in the least. True, there was a fierce expression on his grizzled face, but that expression was always there and had nothing to do with the way Kahlan felt.

Nearby, the surface of the sea was calmer because of a kelp bed which spread a tangled mass of fronds upon the water and softened the fury of the wind. Well within this haven lay Bobry, Kahlan's mate, with their son, Amikuk. Bobry clasped Amikuk to her breast as she floated on her back. Her four feet formed bedposts, and her soft, thick fur was like a coverlet. Amikuk was eighteen inches long; his fur a grizzled brown, his head and neck being rather brindled and his nose and cheeks whitish gray. Bobry was a little over four feet in length and weighed ninety pounds. Her coat was glossy, a brownish black frosted with white-tipped hair, her head and neck grayish white. Like Kahlan's her face was wrinkled in a fierce expression which did not go at all with the pleasant dream she was having.

The forefathers of Kahlan and Bobry had not lived out on the ocean braving the wind and the waves; they had lived on land and had visited the sea only to seek food or to sport in the surf. It was the wonderful robe every otter possessed that had changed their way of life. For centuries the pelt of the sea otter had been the most highly priced fur in the world. Chinese princes paid fabulous prices for the fur, and it was sought after by kings and queens. As recently as 1920 prime pelts brought up to $2,500 each in the London fur sales. In the days before the coming of white hunters to the Aleutian Islands, there were thousands of sea otters living on the rocky shores happy and unafraid.

A stinging sheet of spray swept over mother and baby. Amikuk whimpered and snuggled deeper into his soft bed. But no matter how hard he pushed with his small paws he could not penetrate his mother's thick fur. A sea otter's skin may be stretched to six feet when dried, and still a finger cannot be pushed through the fur to the skin.

Because of its wonderful robe, the sea otter had become a prized trophy for hunters who knew its value. In the year 1742 Vitus Bering's exploring ship was wrecked on the rocky shore of an Alaskan island. Here the explorer died, and his men stayed for months recovering from scurvy. In their search for fresh meat, the sailors came upon the bands of sea otters. It is related that upon finding such a quantity of priceless fur, the men took heart and built a small boat from the wreckage of their ship so that they could take back with them some of the otter skins. Among the survivors was a German naturalist named Steller, who made a detailed report on the sea otters. Without his report we would know very little about the way of life of the otters at that time.

Steller tells how the sea otters gamboled and played and slept on the rocky shores, fearing none but a few of their neighbors. They were intelligent animals filled with a great curiosity about visitors. They welcomed the upright-walking animals and made no attempt to escape when approached. The visitors clubbed seven hundred of the otters to death and took their skins. They would have killed more, but their little boat could not carry a bigger load. They put out to sea and made a safe passage to Siberia. The news of their discovery brought swarms of hunters to the bleak shores where the sea otters lived.

So great was the greed of the hunters who followed Bering that the shameful work of extermination was all but finished in one quarter of the time it took the pioneers to exterminate the buffalo on the American plains. Many islands that had swarmed with otters were without a single otter within five years. Even after Kahlan's forefathers took to the sea, the hunters pursued them and killed them wherever they were found.

The quest of the sea otters caused the Russians to settle Alaska and a new empire was founded. When there were no more otters, the Russians discovered the fur seal, and the scene of slaughter shifted to the Pribilof Islands. A few otters escaped, but their way of life changed; they were still sought after and killed when sighted.

And so Kahlan and Bobry were not friendly, trusting animals like their ancestors. They were shy and watchful, having learned that man was their deadliest enemy. There were other enemies, but they had always been able to cope with them. Against men armed with spears and guns, they were helpless. It made no difference to them that a different sort of man had now appeared who were trying to protect them. They still feared men and chose to live in the midst of the worst weather and the roughest seas rather than risk meeting the poachers who were eager to kill them.

Two hundred years had passed since Kahlan's kind had taken to the sea; in that time they had become sea animals as truly as the whale, more so than the seal tribe. Amikuk had been born at sea while baby seals were born on rocky shores. They had to save themselves, and their only hope lay in the arms of the angry sea.

Kahlan's tribe was the only one of a family of hunters to leave the land and go down to the sea. He belonged to the weasel family known to the scientists as Mustelidae, bloodthirsty bandits feared and hated by other wild animals. His nearest kin was the land otter, which is not so savage a killer as the wolverine, the weasel, the fisher, or the mink and marten. This land cousin was smaller, measuring about three feet in length and only weighing about twenty pounds, but he was a lover of water and a great swimmer and fisherman. Unlike Kahlan he lived on land and liked deep forests where there were many streams.

Perhaps it was because Kahlan's tribe were gentle and fun-loving that they turned their backs upon the others and sought a less bloody way of life, that of fishermen. It may have been that in the past a pair of land otters had gone down to the sea and liked the life there so well that they stayed and taught their children to love the sea. The bitter cold and the stormy weather made it necessary to have a very warm robe, so the otters came to wear a snug waterproof coat of fur. Being so much at sea they developed webbed hind feet, and they grew bigger and stronger because the elements were so savage and unfriendly.

2 : THE WAY OF A FISHERMAN

Kahlan seemed to be sound asleep, but he wasn't completely unconscious of what went on around him. Any otter who slept that soundly would wake up to find himself in the jaws of a killer whale or the maw of a sea lion. Or he might be awakened by the spear of a native hunter.

Bobry slept more soundly, knowing that Kahlan would be watchful. Amikuk just slept, not having a care in his furry head. Nothing worried him except his stomach. He always set up a loud wail when he was hungry. Very soon he would begin to notice things, and his mother would start teaching him what he must know to survive.

It was Amikuk who wakened the family. He opened his big, dark eyes and stared up at the black fog scudding low overhead. He listened to the howling of the wind and the crashing of the waves as they beat against Black Reef. He was snug and warm but his stomach was asking for food. He kicked lustily and gave voice to a loud wail. The wind whipped his voice away instantly. He tried to cry louder and kicked harder. Instantly his mother was awake. She made soothing sounds and kissed him as a human mother would kiss her baby. Amikuk refused to be quieted so she let him nurse. He snuggled down and fed greedily while she lay staring up into the sky.

Out in the rough water, Kahlan raised his head and looked around. The fog had lifted enough so that he could see Black Reef. He moved his hind feet lazily and slid toward the kelp bed. When he was close to Bobry, he raised himself out of the water and looked down at her. He wanted her to join him in a hunt for sea urchins. She splashed her webbed feet and hugged Amikuk closer.

Kahlan was disappointed, but he did not show it. He slid back into the water and lay on his back. Most of his time was spent that way, and he could swim swiftly forward or back without turning over. It was his powerful webbed feet that drove him through the water and steered his course. His forepaws were used as hands, and he could do many wonderful and clever things with them, but they weren't much help in swimming. He plucked a ball of kelp and tossed it into the air. The kelp ball was filled with air, and the wind whipped it away. He found another and tossed it up. This time he caught it. He played this game until Amikuk had finished his dinner.

Amikuk wanted to play after he had finished eating, but his mother placed him on a broad frond and tied him there with strands of kelp. When she was satisfied that he could not fall off the frond, she kicked strongly with her webbed feet and moved out of the kelp bed. Kahlan met her, and they headed for open water, their backs to the deep, their shining breasts to the sky. They moved with easy sinuous sweeps through the mountainous waves, flipping through the troughs and hitting the green wall ahead, shooting through it and leaping upward. Suddenly they both turned, and with backs up like a beaver or a seal, they dived. Strings of silver bubbles drifted upward, marking their course. As the light changed, their black backs became as yellow-brown as a seaman's slicker. Down they went side by side until they reached a submerged reef eighty feet below the surface. They did not need to hurry because they could stay underwater a full five minutes. Groping in the dark, they each located a fat sea urchin. There was little trouble in finding one because the reef teemed with marine life. Strange fishes floated by in schools. They did not linger after securing their catch. Upward they darted and passed through shoals of cod and herring as they neared the surface. A shark swirled lazily but did not strike.

They broke water and lay on their backs, using their breasts as dinner plates. Few animals can smash the spine-covered armor plate of a sea urchin, but Kahlan and Bobry's calloused paws tore open the shell easily. They ate the meat out of the half shell as daintily as a squirrel would pick the meat from a hickory nut. They ate hungrily and spat out bits of pink shell as they munched on the meat. Kahlan finished one half-shell and tossed it far out across the water before starting on the remaining half. Bobry was a little slower, but soon her empty shell sailed over the waves. As soon as they had devoured the meat in the remaining shells, they dived again, and the silver bubbles swirled upward, marking their pathway.

Between dives, both Kahlan and Bobry kept an eye on Amikuk, who was not pleased at being left tied to a frond while his parents enjoyed themselves. Munching and spitting bits of shell, they ignored his wimpering. The waves tossed them and the currents pulled at them, but they were so expert with their webbed feet that they were able to defeat the undertow and the currents. Black Reef, looming only a few yards away, did not worry them at all.

When they had eaten all they wanted, they rolled over to wash the crumbs from their breasts. Then each pulled a soft piece of soapy frond and began lathering their bodies. They did a very careful job, washing their faces, necks, and under their arms, not missing a single part of their bodies. When they were thoroughly soaped, they dived gleefully and came up splashing as they rinsed away the soap.

By now Amikuk was setting up a loud wail and kicking as lustily as he was able. His voice was very much like the voice of a human baby. Bobry paddled to his side and released him from the frond. She tossed him into the air a few times and caught him as he dropped toward her chest; then she hugged and kissed him. Amikuk was restored to good humor. Kahlan moved close to them. He was very fond of his sleek wife and little son. He stroked Bobry, using his forepaws as hands. She pretended not to notice him, giving all her attention to Amikuk.

It was this deep affection between parents and little ones that had proved fatal for otters many times in the past. The hunters would catch a baby, and the mother and father would both die rather than abandon the little one. A mother with her baby clasped to her breast dared not dive to seek the safety of a fog bank because the baby could not live underwater; the mother would die rather than escape without her young one.

Once in a while, Kahlan would land upon the black rocks of the reef as though drawn by some faint yearning out of the past. But if there was the faintest taint of campfire smoke in the air, even the taint of a fire five miles away, or if there was the lingering taint of a man track, he would rush back to the sea. The man track might be washed by many waves and rain squalls, but if there was any trace left it would be enough to fill the otter with panic.

Black Reef was not inaccessible to the Aleut hunters who lived on the mainland, and who lived off the sea as much as the otters did. The Aleuts were masters of rough water, too. In their skin boats, called bidarkees, they braved the worst gales and the most turbulent seas. The skin covering of their boats had two holes in it. An Aleut sat in each hole and laced the skin top tight around him so that the bidarkee would not fill with water if it turned over. Thus the bidarkee became a part of the two hunters. The Aleuts seldom visited Black Reef because they were no longer allowed to hunt sea otters.

None of this bothered Kahlan and Bobry at the moment, and it certainly did not bother Amikuk as he played on his mother's breast. He would one day be a great swimmer like his father, but at this stage he would have sunk like a bit of water-logged wood had he fallen into the water. He would have to learn to swim just as a young bird learns to fly. Bobry knew this, and she believed in starting to teach him while he was young. She caught him up, and he squealed gleefully. His cry of glee changed to one of fear when she tossed him into the water. He kicked and spluttered and sank. Bobry quickly caught him and lifted him out of the water, shaking the briny drops from his fur, then snuggled him close to her.

Kahlan circled about, a worried look on his wrinkled face. He was not a fierce fellow; he just looked like a grumpy old man. His whiskers always bristled and his expression was always that of an angry fellow. Bobry thought him very fine looking. She knew he was seldom angry though he could show temper when seagulls tried to steal his dinner from him.

Amikuk lay looking up into the sky. The gale

which had for hours lashed the coast had slackened, but the wind was still stirring in a gusty and uncertain fashion. In all of its history this barren coast had never known a full day's calm. Strangely enough, the bitter cold of the arctic never descended upon the island chain. This was summer weather with the temperature hovering close to fifty degrees above zero. Even in winter the temperature would seldom drop below thirty degrees at sea level. But winter or summer, there was always fog and wind.

A chattering flock of little auks swept low over the water. These bright and fearless little sparrows of the north swirled above the family floating on the waves. Amikuk sat up and lifted his paws, but none of the birds dipped low enough for him to catch it. The flock whirled upward on a gust of wind and was gone, vanishing into a bank of fog.

Amikuk watched for other birds. Soon a white gull of the north swept low over the reef. This gull was big, and its wings spread wide. It banked and dived as it studied the otter family. Deciding there was nothing to eat below, it turned gracefully and let an updraft of air sweep it away. Amikuk made a game out of watching the gulls as they flew and dived.

He was rudely awakened from this game by a sudden movement of his mother. His father, too, had changed, sinking now into the water until only his nose showed. Amikuk looked out over the churning waves. He sensed the sudden fear that had taken hold of his mother, but he did not see anything. Out in the open water, three tall black fins were cutting the waves at great speed. They were bearing down upon the little bay where the family rested. Suddenly Kahlan dived and was gone. Amikuk kicked his legs eagerly and squirmed, thinking this must be a new game.

Bobry knew it was no game. She knew she should dive deep and come up within the shelter of the kelp bed. She also knew that if she dived and did not come up until she reached the kelp bed that Amikuk would smother. She gave two powerful thrusts with her webbed feet and shot away at top speed. Her eyes checked the distance to the kelp bed, and then she turned to check the onrushing dorsal fins. Those fins belonged to three killer whales, twenty-foot terrors armed with ragged teeth and capable of terrific speed. Nothing that swam was safe from the killer whales, not even the biggest whale, three times the length and thirty times the weight of the killers. The three tall fins swerved, and Bobry knew the pack had sighted her and were closing in for the kill, each eager to snatch the prize.

Her eyes darted to the kelp bed with its tangled mass of fronds and ropes. The killers would not dare to penetrate the jungle of seaweed, but she could not reach that haven; the distance was too great. Kahlan, who should have been safe among the kelp, arose beside her. He would not desert her, though there was nothing he could do to help her.

Her eyes turned back to her pursuers, and she saw a great head rise out of the water. A huge mouth opened and hissing foam sprayed over ragged teeth. Small pig-eyes gleamed madly as the killer prepared to strike. Bobry had only one trick left, a desperate chance, but all she could do. She stopped swimming and let her body float while she clasped Amikuk tightly against her breast to keep him from whimpering. He, too, must lie motionless; there must be no live movement for the little pig-eyes to catch. At her side Kahlan was floating like a water-soaked log. Both drifted aimlessly, whirled this way and that by the currents and lifted by the waves.

Amikuk had seen the gaping jaws of the killer and had set up a loud wail. When his mouth was stopped by her warm fur, he burrowed deep and clung to her. Side by side, Kahlan and Bobry floated until a current caught them and pulled them toward the black rocks of the reef. They made no effort to fight against the pull of the green water.

The killers came on at a terrific pace. Great heads lifted, and little eyes searched for the escaping prey. They saw two floating bodies, but the killer whales never ate carrion; they devoured only kills they made themselves. Their small brains were not able to understand the trick being played upon them. They plunged past Kahlan and Bobry, seeking the living otters that had seemingly vanished from the sea. Nearing the kelps beds, they swerved and swam along the reef, then headed back out to sea.

Amikuk felt his mother's arms loosen and squirmed enough to be able to turn his head. The terrifying beasts were gone but towering above him were ragged, black rocks with spray foaming over them. Water surged in and out of channels between the rocks. He was sure his mother would be smashed upon the rocks. He could feel her body strain against the pull of the water. For an instant he caught a glimpse of his father riding the top of a big wave that was about to smash upon the rocks. Then everything was blotted out as Bobry dived through a big wave. Amikuk sputtered and choked and tried to cry out, but the air was so full of the roaring of the surf that he could not make himself heard. For a moment his mother rode the next wave before she dived again. Seconds later she was clear of the sucking currents and headed for the kelp bed. Amikuk sputtered and coughed as he cleared the water from his throat and lungs.

Then Kahlan came shooting along and glided at Bobry's side. He had escaped from the pull of the current by darting between two big rocks and then riding the returning wall of water back out to sea. Mother and father did not slow their pace until they were well within the kelp bed. When they were secure from attack by the killer whales—should they return—they lay close together with the kelp fronds hiding their bodies. Only their big watchful eyes and their snouts were exposed.

When tall black fins had not come back after an hour of hiding, they kicked aside the kelp and floated in a small pool which was clear of fronds. With them, fear was a passing shadow and when that shadow vanished, they soon forgot about the danger. Kahlan began tossing a kelp float while Bobry played with Amikuk, mixing his play with bits of learning he would need later. His schooling would take most of a year, and during that time Amikuk would need his mother. He would not be able to live without her.

3 : PETER

Peter lay on a rocky ledge far out on Black Reef. His body was protected from the wind by a slab of stone which rose high above him. When a great wave smashed against the base of the ledge, white spume swirled over him, and sometimes salty spray spattered him. He did not come to this rocky ledge to look for eggs of the arrie or to net little auks or to seek precious driftwood for the little iron stove in his father's hut. No one climbed so far out along the rocky barrier except Peter, and he could not have explained in words why he made such a desperate journey. The thoughts which filled his head as he lay looking out over the water were foolish thoughts—he was sure of that—but they were also wonderful thoughts.

To reach his lookout point he had to slip along

narrow ribs of stone, leaping forward when a great wave receded baring his path, clinging to jutting shoulders of slippery stone when the green wall rushed back, always keeping just out of reach of the angry waves. It was a dangerous feat, one that filled him with excitement. Peter had lived all of his twelve years so close to the wild water that he could not remember a time when the boom of the surf had not been in his ears. The ocean furnished most of his food and clothing, and he was as much at home in his little kayak, paddling through stormy seas, as he was climbing the cliffs which rose above his home.

Peter was watching a family of sea otters playing near a kelp bed. There was a mother and a father and a little one. This family stayed close to the reef so that he was able to observe them even on foggy days. They were the first sea otters he had ever been able to watch. They fascinated him and filled his head with eager pictures. In a way they reminded him of his own family. In his family there was his father, Kahgo, his mother, Saan, and himself. He could remember his mother playing with him the way the mother otter played with the little one, and the father otter reminded him of his father, who always looked grim and was ever silent though he was fond of Saan and of Peter.

The first time he had seen the otters floating so close to shore, he had wanted to run home and tell his father about them. Two otter skins would bring a lot of money. They would be worth more than all of the fox skins his father took in a whole year. But he had not told his father because the Aleuts were no longer allowed to kill otters. His mother had explained it to him. Any hunter who killed an otter would be punished. His father said this was not right or just, that things of the sea belonged to the people; it had always been that way. His father and the other hunters were seldom tempted to break the law because there were few otters left and sighting one was a rare occurrence. The trader in the village would not buy otter skins, but when a hunter took one it could be sold to strangers who came across the water from Siberia during the summer.

Peter came often to the ledge to watch the otters, and his head was always filled with dreams. He had listened many times to the tales the old men told of the days when the men were allowed to hunt sea otters. Most of the nice things in his home had been bought with money his grandfather had gotten for otter pelts. Now they never had any new things. The fox pelts brought just enough in trade to furnish sugar and tea and a little cloth.

The old men's tales of hunting the otters always facinated Peter. It had been dangerous and exciting sport. Surf clubbing had been the most dangerous of all. The hunters would brave wind so strong a man could not stand against it. This wind lashed the ocean into mountainous waves which smashed upon the shore. Two hunters would crouch under the shelter of a bluff, and from this shelter they would launch their bidarkee. Firmly laced into their boat, they would send it darting into the wild waves like an arrow before the wind. Their goal would be a series of islets some twenty miles away. The hunters must approach with the storm if they were to surprise the otters. While the storm raged, the otters would seek shelter on the lee side of an island, above the wash of the surf where they would lie with their heads buried in seaweed. The hunters could approach unheard because of the roaring of the storm and bludgeon the otters with clubs without alarming any except those attacked.

The danger lay in braving an arctic storm in a flimsy skin boat. The bidarkees were often tossed into the air and turned over, but the skillful boatmen simply righted them again and shook the water out of their eyes and off their clothing, then plunged into the next wave.

And there was the "surround," a chase for

calmer weather. Many boats set out, and when an otter was sighted, it was surrounded. Spears flashed, and the otter dived to remain submerged for about five minutes. Each time the otter appeared, the spears were hurled, and there was much shouting and smashing of oars upon the water so that the little beast never had time to take a full breath of air. In the end, the otter was unable to stay underwater at all and was impaled upon a spear. Peter felt he had missed a great deal by being born after the otters had vanished.

Watching the otter family, Peter worked out a plan for taking at least one of them. He got the idea from the stories he had heard and from watching the family below his lookout. When the mother and father moved to deep water to dive for sea urchins, they always left the baby moored to a kelp frond. The old man had said that if a hunter caught a baby otter, the mother and the father would swim to his boat, and he could kill at least one of them with a club. He had no idea how he would be able to sell an otter pelt, but this did not bother him. He would settle that later.

Peter was always careful not to let the otters see him. He knew they would seek another kelp bed if they knew he was watching them. The day his plan came to him, he lingered on the ledge longer than usual, and when he started back the rising tide made the trip dangerous. He darted and leaped and clung to the wet rocks, fighting his way slowly toward shore. The chilly water soaked him and the spray stung his face. He was panting and shaken when he reached the mainland, and seated himself on a rock to catch his breath.

He must find at least a small bundle of driftwood to take back with him. More fortunate families could afford to buy cordwood or coal, but not his family. They depended upon driftwood and bundles of crowberry vines which his mother gathered from the crags above the hut. Peter walked slowly along the shore, looking for pieces of wood cast up by the waves. He was lucky to find a battered log wedged between two rocks. It was water-soaked, but he was able to drag it out of the rocks and pull it along the beach.

Summer was the best time of the year for the family. During the summer, many birds nested on the crags and cliffs. The eggs of the arrie were gaily colored and good to eat and were plentiful. Little auks could be netted, and there were a few berries which grew in sheltered spots. During the summer, the family did not depend so much upon the ocean for food. Peter moved slowly because the log was heavy. Looking up at the cliffs he wished the summer would never end.

Peter's home was a one-room hut. His grandfather had built it, and it now belonged to Kahgo and Saan. His father, like his grandfather, had never wanted to live in the village which was a mile from the hut. The hut was called a barrabora and had been built by excavating a cellar three feet deep and twelve feet square, over which a driftwood frame had been erected. This frame was covered with cut bog peet and the earth from the excavation. The walls were two feet thick. The entrance was through a small door leading into a little hallway made of peat and sod. Another small door opened from the hallway into the main room, which was separated into two parts by a curtain of cotton cloth. The floor was hard-packed earth, and there was a little iron stove with a stovepipe. In the living room, there was a low table and a few wooden boxes for chairs. Back of the curtain stood two beds, a narrow one for Peter and a wide one for his mother and father. The beds were bunks with thick feather-stuffed mattresses on them.

Peter left the log outside and entered the barrabora. His father was seated on a box, and his mother was stirring the contents of a kettle simmering on the stove. Peter paused when he saw sugar and tea on the table; that meant company. Turning his head, he looked at the visitor. He was a short broad-shouldered man with slanting eyes and a skin much lighter than that of an Aleut. The stranger had stopped talking to Peter's father when Peter entered. He looked at the boy out of black eyes and smiled. Kahgo spoke slowly.

"My son, Peter," he said.

"I am Ivan," the stranger said, and his smiled spread.

Peter glanced at his mother and saw that there was a frown on her lips. He sensed that she did not like this man, Ivan. He moved to a corner and sat down, wondering what the stranger wanted.

"Did you find wood?" his mother asked.

"A good log," Peter answered. He wasn't really listening to his mother; he was interested in the talk between his father and the stranger. He caught a note of anger in his father's voice.

"I do not hunt the otter," Kahgo said. "But it is my right to take otters if I wish to hunt them."

"You are distant from the village, and I will buy any skins you take," Ivan said. "There are so few that the price is very high."

Peter felt a sudden surge of excitement, but his father's words were not encouraging.

"It would mean bad trouble for me. I will not look for otters."

"That is true," Saan said. "Hunting the otters would bring trouble to us."

Ivan did not say any more. He ate the boiled cod that Saan set before him and drank tea. The talk was about other things. Peter hurried through his meal and left the hut. He sat on the drift log and looked out to sea. A very exciting idea was forming in his head. It frightened him, but he could not stop thinking about it. He fixed his eyes on Ivan's skin boat and frowned fiercely. After a time, he got to his feet and walked down to the landing rocks.

Later Ivan appeared, but Peter's father did not come out of the hut. Ivan walked down to the landing. He smiled at Peter and shook his head.

"Your father is a stubborn man, but perhaps I will have better luck in the village."

"I could get one—I might get two otters," Peter said. "No one would know."

Ivan turned back from his boat. "If you can, there will be much money for you and your family," he said.

Peter nodded. "My mother needs a new dress. We are very poor."

"I will return. If you take skins, hide them near the shore. I will look at them and pay you for them." Ivan glanced toward the hut, then got into his boat.

Peter said, "I promise at least one skin."

Ivan nodded and shoved off, dipping his paddle expertly. Peter stood watching him move away and was suddenly frightened at what he had said.

4 : PLANS

Amikuk's lessons in swim-
ming were progressing daily. At first he sank like a
stone when Bobry tossed him into the water, but he
always struggled and kicked, and she always rescued him before he swallowed too much water.
After each ducking he would lie on her broad breast
and make angry, protesting sounds. His efforts in
kicking showed him that he could keep himself
afloat with his hind flippers. This was the first step
toward paddling. It was not very successful and he
had to be rescued each time, but as he learned to
keep afloat, he found he liked the water.

Being able to swim even a little opened a new
world for him, though he was not allowed to explore much of it; his mother stayed close to him
when they were in the open water, and when she
left him he was always tied securely to a kelp frond.

He objected very much to being tied up, but she knew best what was safe for him. After each dive—before she settled down to enjoy her catch—she would rise out of the water and make sure that he was firmly bound to the kelp.

His diet of milk was enlarged to include bits of sea urchin, clam, cuttlefish, or limpit—whatever his mother was having for dinner. At first he spat the bits of meat out of his mouth, but soon he was chewing eagerly upon them and demanding more. It would be months before he would hunt for his own food, but his mother wanted him to acquire a taste for the good things the ocean had to offer. This was an important part of his education.

His father was becoming restless. Kahlan was eager for the day when the baby would be able to travel, and they could take trips, and adventure along the fringes of the kelp beds. He favored one spot as home, but his range of rough water was some sixty miles, and his active body demanded an outlet for its energy. It was not that there was any lack of food or need to seek a new hunting ground. As for Bobry, she was in no hurry. She was concerned only with the safety of her baby, and in seeing to it that he could take care of himself on the storm-harassed coast. She felt safe in the cove with the protecting kelp beds nearby.

Finally a day came when she decided Amikuk swam well enough to play a game of water tag. She pushed Amikuk into the water. As soon as he was paddling strongly, she swam in a circle. He paddled after her as fast as he could, and she set a pace which kept her just ahead of him. Amikuk sputtered and scolded to make her wait for him, but she kept on swimming until he was so out of breath that he had to stop. The moment he ceased paddling, he sank under the water. She turned sharply and dived, catching him by his neck fur and lifting him clear of the water. She lifted him high and shook the water from his fur, all the while making encouraging noises to soothe his anger. She placed him on top of her and smoothed his fur. Kahlan had been watching the lesson carefully and now he moved in close. He was hungry and wanted to swim out to deep water where he could dive for sea urchins but he wanted Bobry to come too.

Amikuk fussed and fretted for a while. He was not nearly so peeved as he acted. He had rather liked the game, but by fretting he could get more attention from his mother. Finally he settled down, intending to take a nap. The moment he closed his eyes, Bobry gave two strong strokes with her flippers and glided to the kelp bed. He could sleep just as well anchored to a kelp frond as on her breast, and she was hungry. He protested sleepily when she wrapped a strand of kelp around him but he did not struggle. As soon as he was securely tied, she darted away to join Kahlan.

A heavy sea was running, piled high by lashing wind, and the coming storm quickened their pulses. It was always in rough weather that the otters felt the greatest urge to play and frolic. Away Bobry darted, diving through big waves, whirling and twisting and ducking back and forth. Kahlan swam close behind her, matching her long leaps when she shot out of a wave. He was not superior to her in speed or strength—they were the same size and weight—nor did their color or markings differ. They ended the race by wrestling wildly and ducking each other vigorously. Kahlan added a special touch by placing his forepaws on the knees of his hind flippers and doubling into a ball. Over and over he spun like a pinwheel, doing thirty or more spins before he darted back to where Bobry lay watching him.

From his hidding place on the reef, Peter watched the pair at play and laughed softly as Kahlan made the water fly while he was pinwheeling over the waves. The otters had more fun than he had, he decided wistfully. They never had to worry about food or clothing, they were always warm and dry. Living alone with his father and mother, he had no other boys to play with. When he had asked his mother why they lived so far from the village, she had explained that they could not afford to build a barrabora of their own. Kahgo's father had given them his hut. Perhaps someday, if they could save a little money, they would build a home in the village.

When the mother and father otters started diving, Peter gave his attention to the baby. Thinking about being able to afford a house in the village made him eager to complete his plans for taking the otters. In a day or two he would paddle his little kayak to a spot at the foot of the rock wall where he lay. All he was waiting for was to have the weather settle so that his hunt would have the best chance to succeed, and he was sure a calmer day would come very soon.

Out in the deep water, Kahlan and Bobry had finished a meal. They moved lazily toward the reef where it was overgrown with seaweed. They had decided they wanted a change of fare. Among the tangled weeds, they found snails, clams, and a variety of crustaceans. Selecting choice morsels, they ate them without hurry. Finally Bobry darted off to care for her baby. Kahlan secured two fat crabs and lingered to eat them.

PLANS

Amikuk was awake and peevish when Bobry arrived at the kelp bed. He let his mother know he felt she had been neglecting him. She removed him from the frond and cuddled him and played with him until his good humor was restored, then she floated on her back and they both took a nap.

Peter slipped away from his hiding place and returned to the mainland. His head was full of the many things he would do with the money that he would get for the otter skins. When he reached the hut, he slipped around behind it and sat on a rock while he sharpened his hunting knife. It was an old knife that his father had given him. The handle was broken and the blade worn thin by repeated sharpenings. The otters must be skinned carefully so that Ivan would be pleased with the pelts. Peter knew how to remove the skins, having helped his mother skin seals and sea lions and his father skin foxes. He worked upon the blade with a piece of sandstone until the edge and the point were keen. Testing the blade on his thumbnail he decided the edge was as sharp as he could get it. He hid the knife in a hole in the wall of the hut and walked to the front of the house.

A glance inside the hut told him there was no one home. His father was probably at the village and his mother up on the cliffs gathering fuel and berries. He knew he should go hunt for wood. A glance at the sky told him that tomorrow might be a good day with not too much wind. The storm was showing signs of blowing itself out. Overhead the birds were on the wing, able to master the wind and eager to fly. That, too, was a good sign.

But he did not go down to the beach to look for driftwood. Instead, he searched in a pile of poles used for drying fish and found a piece of heavy wood some three feet in length. He took it around to the back of the hut and pulled his knife from its hiding place, then seated himself and started whittling a club. He had seen clubs used for killing otters and knew that they were shaped so that one end was heavy and blunt while the other formed a good handhold. When the club was finished, he hid it along with the knife under a flat stone some distance from the hut.

Peter was already beginning to think of hunting wood as a waste of time. After he got the money from Ivan, they could buy fuel. He sauntered down toward the beach, his head full of plans for a new home, cloth for his mother, a new knife, possibly even a cheap rifle. Other hunters who had sold skins to men like Ivan had been able to buy such things.

He wandered along, not watching very closely

for driftwood. It was not until he started back that he really searched the beach and was able to bring in a few battered pieces of ship timber. As he approached the hut, he saw his mother coming down the path from the cliffs. She had a big bundle of crowberry vines on her head, and the weight made her stoop far over. Peter frowned. The village women no longer struggled under loads of vines. She wouldn't have to do it after he had gotten the money. As he tossed his armload of wood down beside the door, he felt ashamed because it was such a small bundle.

His mother did not chide him. She gave him a smile as she seated herself and started twisting the vines into short ropes which would make a quick, hot fire when placed in the little iron stove. Along with what driftwood could be found, the vines would have to keep them warm, and his mother was building up a supply against the coming of winter.

Back at the kelp bed in the cove, Amikuk was awake though his mother still slept. He sat on her breast staring out over the waves. When she was lifted high, he could see far out beyond the reef. When she sank down, he could see nothing but a bit of sky and green walls of water.

It was when he was high above the surface that

he saw the strange animal approaching. The animal was many times larger than his mother, measuring eight feet in length and weighing over four hundred pounds. It seemed to be all neck and shoulders with a very small head, and it swam swiftly, straight toward the sleeping Bobry. Amikuk set up a wild cry of fright which made his mother open her eyes at once. He expected her to take him in her mouth and flee in hasty retreat, but all she did was give a powerful thrust with her flippers which sent her shooting off at an angle to the course of the onrushing monster.

Bobry knew the fur seal was not an enemy. The big bull did not even look at her as he moved past, swimming strongly. His face was toward the distant islands of the mist where he would make his summer home. He was not interested in food; his only thought was to reach the islands as soon as possible. He had been swimming steadily for hundreds of miles, and he had many more miles to cover before he would rest. A powerful urge drove him forward and would not let him stop until he had reached the islands and claimed a small plot of rock where he could gather a harem of cow seals around him. He had stopped eating several weeks before and would not touch food for many weeks. The huge shoulders and neck were padded with layers of fat which he would use to sustain him during the months of fasting.

Amikuk watched the big fellow swim away. He was still trembling but soon settled down as he realized he had been in no danger. His mother was not afraid of the big animal, so he need have no fear of it. Soon he slid off into the water and started paddling around her. She stirred herself and played a game of tag with him. Kahlan floated nearby, napping. He had wakened briefly when the seal passed, and then he had gone back to sleep. But as Amikuk and his mother splashed and darted about, he roused himself. After a bit he joined them, splashing Amikuk with spray as he darted past him to take the lead.

After a half hour of tag, Kahlan headed out toward deep water. Bobry coasted to a halt, and Amikuk paddled at her side. Kahlan was trying to lead them off on a cruise beyond the reef. Bobry gave a lazy thrust with one flipper, and coasted toward the kelp bed. It was her answer to his invitation. She was not ready to leave the cove.

Out in the deep water, Kahlan lifted himself above a wave, and looked back. He raised one paw as though to shade his eyes. As he sank back into the water, he knew it was no use; she wasn't ready to leave the kelp beds. He pretended to go on alone but did not move very fast.

A stiff breeze blowing along the coast carried the roars of a herd of sea lions on a rookery a mile to the east. Kahlan hesitated and listened. The baby was too small to be taken near a sea lion rookery. The giants liked otter meat, especially that of the young ones. He turned his head and raised his body high on a wave. A bank of fog had drifted between himself and the cove; he could not see Bobry. With sudden energy, he stroked fast and shot back toward the kelp bed. As he broke through the fog bank, he saw that Bobry was anxiously peering toward the open sea. When he came into view, she lay back and drifted. When he slid to rest beside her, she pretended she didn't know he had returned. She started playing with Amikuk.

5 : THE HUNT

Peter was certain there was nothing wrong with his plans for the hunt. He was a little worried about what his father and mother would say when he showed them the sack of money Ivan would give him. But he was not disobeying his father. Kahgo had never told him not to hunt otters, and he did not think it fair to punish the Aleuts for hunting for valuable skins. He was frowning stubbornly as he tramped down to the shore with his knife and club concealed inside his rainproof jacket.

He did not have to worry about his father asking him where he was going; Kahgo was in the village, probably smoking and talking to the hunters in the community house, and his mother was up near the crags gathering berries for a savory dish she prepared by mixing the tart fruit with fresh blubber. By the time the evening meal was ready, he would have cached away at least one other skin. That thought banished all of his doubts, and he eagerly pushed his kayak toward the water.

He slid into the round hole in the kayak and laced the opening tight around his middle. Placing his club before him, he thrust the two-bladed paddle against a rock and shoved off.

Peter was very proud of his kayak. He had built it himself, except for the stitching, which had been done by his mother. He kept it well oiled so that not a drop of water seeped into it. He was dressed in store clothing except for his boots which were made of sea lion intestines and his waterproof coat which his mother had fashioned from the intestines of a seal. No clothing could equal these when exposed to drenching waves and flying spray. The boys in the village wore store boots and store coats, but his family was too poor to buy them so he wore what his forefathers had always worn.

With a powerful thrust of his paddle, he sent the kayak shooting out into the surf where great waves rushed in to meet his frail craft. To Peter this was a calm day and a gentle sea though the waves rose high above the little boat and tossed it about like a straw. Peter sent it forward, meeting the high waves and riding them with ease.

Looking back he smiled broadly. The hills and

the mountains rising above the mainland were a rich, dark green to the loftiest summits, with only a light patch of snow glistening now and then to relieve the grayish brown of the rocky shingle which marked the highest peaks. A few stunted willows clung to the slopes. They were the only trees that grew on the mainland. They clung to the banks along the rivulets, and the tallest of them was not more than five feet in height.

A more cautious boatman would have stayed well away from the black rocks over which the waves were breaking. Peter's plan called for hugging the shore so that he would not be seen by the otters. He knew they were wary and would be gone at the first sign or scent of a man and a boat. A dense bank of fog rolled in obscuring all rocks more than a few yards away. This suited Peter very well; it would hide his approach if the otters were out near the tip of the reef. He did not worry about being heard because the surf was booming so loudly that the splash of his oars was swallowed up. He was sure the fog would lift very soon. He had the patience of all sea hunters and could wait.

The fog kept pressing down upon the sea and curling over the waves. Peter kept close to the black rocks until he came to the reef which he recognized by the change in direction of the shore line. As he turned inland he moved more slowly and finally found the little inlet he must pass through to reach the base of the cliff where he would lie waiting for the fog to lift. He sent the kayak darting between big rocks and came to calmer water. Here he shoved in close to a shelf and unlaced the opening. Getting out of the kayak he slid it up on the shelf. As he worked, he kept testing the wind to make sure the otters would not catch his scent. Setting his club beside the kayak he climbed slowly up the face of the cliff and stretched out on his lookout point.

An hour passed and the fog continued to funnel along the coast and over the reef. But the wind was freshening, and he was hopeful. He chewed a piece of dried fish he had brought with him and stared into the damp, swirling mist. Then, very suddenly the wind shifted. Peter turned his eyes toward the kelp beds. The fog showed signs of breaking into long streamers and rolling clouds. Within a half an hour he caught a glimpse of the dark mass of kelp awash beyond the reef. A few minutes later he was able to see clearly, and he spotted the otter family floating close to a tangle of fronds. Without moving, he lay waiting for the family to wake up.

As usual Amikuk wakened first and set up a clamor. He was hungry and wanted to be fed at once. His mother opened her eyes, but she did not move. Amikuk's cries grew louder. She stirred and let him nurse. After he had fed, she washed him carefully. Kahlan had roused himself and was watching his family eagerly. It was time for Amikuk's swimming lessons and his mother glided away from the kelp bed with Kahlan swimming at her side. She eased the baby into the water and they started a game of tag.

Upon the high rock Peter felt excitement taking hold of him. Soon the old ones would get hungry and leave the baby while they dived for sea urchins. Easing himself up on his elbows, he waited, his eyes fastened upon the bobbing heads of the otters.

Twice the father started for deep water, but each time he stopped when his mate did not follow him. Finally she swam to the kelp bed and anchored the baby securely to a kelp frond. Peter curbed his impatience. He had to be sure they were going to dive out in deep water and not fish the shore. That would give him time to get his boat and run out to the kelp bed where the baby lay helplessly tied to a frond. The pair swam about lazily at first; then they started a wild game of racing through the waves. This lasted all of a half hour, and Peter began to fear they might not go diving at all. But at last they moved far out and started diving. The moment they were out of sight under the water,

Peter scrambled down the face of the cliff to his boat. He knew he would have at least three minutes to get to the shelf.

Reaching the kayak he lay down beside it and peered over it without exposing himself. He saw the pair surface and float on their backs. They ate slowly, enjoying their meal. At last the final shell was sucked dry and tossed aside. The father and mother dived again, and Peter hastened to lace himself into the kayak and slide it off the shelf. He made sure his club was ready as he sent the boat darting away from the rocks and into open water.

Amikuk saw the kayak bearing down upon him and struggled against the strands of kelp which held him. His big eyes stared up at Peter as the kayak drew near, and he wailed like a baby crying. Peter was so excited he almost ran the little otter down. He turned the kayak broadside and reached down. His hand closed on the neck fur of the little otter, and he shook it free of the kelp strands, then lifted it into the air. Amikuk kicked lustily and called for his mother. Peter held the squirming otter in his left hand while with his right he grasped his club. His eyes were on the deep water out where the parents had dived.

Bobry surfaced first, and the instant she heard the wail of her baby she tossed aside the sea urchin

Bobry and Kahlan surfaced and saw the kayak and the young hunter holding Amikuk.

she had caught. She saw the kayak and the young hunter, but she did not hesitate; she swam directly toward them. She moved with a wild rush of speed, swimming high out of the water, not trying to conceal her body.

Peter gripped his club and waited. His heart was pounding hard, and his breath was coming fast. On came the mother, her big eyes wild with fear, her cry rising above the distant roar of the surf. She was doing just what the old men had said a mother otter would do, and her mate was following her, swimming close behind her.

Peter got a firmer grip on the little one. A thought struck him. What would he do with the little one after he had killed the mother? He did not have time to decide before the mother reached the kayak's side. She raised herself out of the water and reached for her baby with both forepaws. Peter looked down at her as he raised his club. He could not miss her round furry head. One blow would stun her and then he could finish her. He did not see her bristling face with its always angry look, all he saw was her big pleading eyes. He did not strike, and he was not able to think why he could not smash her skull. He wet his lips and leaned far over the side of the kayak, but he did not strike. His arm seemed paralyzed, and he had a sick feeling at the pit of his stomach.

Something close to a sob slipped through his lips as he slowly lowered the club. He couldn't kill her. It would be like hitting his own mother. Before he had time to give the matter any thought at all, he lowered the baby and dropped it gently into the water. Instantly the mother caught it with her teeth and darted away.

Peter sat watching the otters as they swam toward open water. The mother was now swimming on her back with her baby clasped to her breast, the father swam well back and kept looking toward

Peter as though expecting to be followed. When they reached the point of the reef they turned east and disappeared from sight.

Peter knew that he would never dare tell anyone what he had done. The hunters would laugh at him, and the boys would taunt him. He was no hunter, just a girl afraid of a little blood. But he was glad the otters had escaped. He remembered hearing the men say that no one had ever been able to raise a baby otter. The little ones always died when they were separated from their mothers.

He sat for a long time staring toward the fog bank where the otters had vanished. Slowly the realization came to him that he had watched the family so many times that he had come to think of them more as people than animals. He had enjoyed their games, even envied the fun they had. He had, in a way, shared their affection for each other. They had become his friends and one does not kill a friend. Having thought it through, he felt much better. Perhaps it was not right to kill otters. And now he was sorry he had given them such a fright. They would leave and he would never see them again.

He dipped his paddle and headed the kayak toward home. Knowing he would need an excuse for going out in the boat, he turned into a small cove and uncoiled his fish line. Within a half-hour, he had landed a fat halibut which would furnish more than one meal for the family. He paddled slowly home and beached his boat. His mother was seated on a stone before the hut mixing berries and oil in a bowl. Peter got out of the kayak and carried the fish to the hut. His mother smiled up at him as he held up his catch.

"You have caught a fine fish," she said.

Peter laid the halibut on a flat stone and sat down on the ground. He looked about for his father but did not see him.

"I am worried about your father," Saan said. "He has been talking with Old Luca about otter hunting. It is that man—Ivan. He is wicked and will lead our men into much trouble."

Peter smiled. He was sure there was one family of otters they would not find very quickly. His mother frowned, thinking he was smiling at her worries.

"There could be much trouble," she said.

"I do not think they can find any otters," Peter said.

"Your father said he saw a pair just off Black Reef." Saan gave the oil a final whip and got to her feet. "Perhaps I worry too much."

"I will help father repair the fox traps and ask him to go with me netting little auks," Peter said.

"You are a good boy." Saan picked up the fish and the bowl of berries and oil.

Peter knew as he watched his mother enter the hut that she would have been very unhappy if he had killed the otters. Suddenly the money did not seem important. He got to his feet and entered the hut.

Kahgo arrived while Saan was broiling the halibut steaks. He sniffed eagerly as he seated himself on a box.

"Peter caught a fine fish," Saan explained.

"And you have been picking berries." Kahgo smiled at his wife.

She looked anxiously at him. "What did you hear in the village?"

"The hunters are restless. Old Luca says he will take any otters he can find." Kahgo's smile faded.

"And what does the government man say?" Saan asked.

"He says we must wait. He says we must let the otters live and that some day we may hunt them again." Kagho shook his head. "I do not agree."

"I think he speaks the truth," Peter said.

Kahgo gave his son a surprised look. "What would you know about otters?" he asked sharply.

"You must wait," Peter's mother said firmly.

"The government man will leave soon and be

gone a long time," Kahgo said. "There would be no danger of being caught if only a few otters were taken, and the hunters would be lucky to find more than one pair."

Peter glanced at his father and knew he was troubled. He had a feeling his father had promised to hunt with Old Luca or at least he had promised to lead him to the pair of otters living near Black Reef. Ivan must have been talking with Old Luca. Peter smiled. The otters would not be at Black Reef when the men went there seeking them. Then his smile faded. He knew the hunters would paddle quite a distance along the coast, and he was not sure the otter family would move very far.

6 : A NEW HOME

Bobry refused to travel far in their flight from Black Reef. Her meeting with the young hunter had been terrifying, but the dreaded enemy had not harmed her or her baby, even though she had been very close to him, so close he could have killed her and so close the man smell had been powerful. Amikuk was too young and weak to make a long trip. She dreaded the open sea with its killer whales and sharks and sea lions. She knew she was helpless so long as he was too young to stay underwater. She was looking for kelp beds and meant to stop as soon as they came to one.

Kahlan would have kept on moving eastward along the chain of islands, but Bobry turned toward shore at the first reef which sheltered a kelp bed. She swam into the jungle of fronds and refused to leave it. He called from open water and coaxed, but she refused to leave the kelp. After trying for almost an hour he gave up and joined her. She and Amikuk took a long nap, but he remained awake and watchful, floating with only his muzzle and eyes above water. Though no enemy appeared, he did not lessen his vigilance.

The new home was much like the one they had left. There was a reef extending out from the mainland, and down some sixty feet there was a submerged reef which teemed with sea urchins; close to shore there was a mass of seaweed. This was an ideal home, but it bothered Kahlan that they had not fled very far.

Amikuk was beginning to swim more strongly. His awkward paddling was changing to swifter, surer strokes which allowed him to maneuver more freely. When he played tag with his mother, he was able to duck and swerve by using his flippers. One day he followed his mother through a big wave and liked the trick so well he kept diving through waves until he was exhausted. Plunging through the green wall of water taught him how to hold his breath when submerged, and this led to shallow dives and an introduction to a world he had not known existed.

One day he tried to follow his mother down to the

submerged reef. She and Kahlan went down swiftly, and he struggled to follow them. Down he went into the green water paddling furiously, but unable to keep pace with his mother. He almost collided with a large fish and this so frightened him that he opened his mouth to call for his mother. Instantly he swallowed water and started choking. Thrashing wildly, he arose and popped out of the water choking and sputtering. Instinctively he swam to the kelp bed where he lay on a mass of fronds until the water was out of his lungs.

When Bobry and Kahlan surfaced with their sea urchins, he had recovered enough to swim out to her and demand a share of her dinner. She shared her catch with him, and they finished the meat quickly. She dived again but he did not try to follow her. He had learned that monsters lived in the world below. The one he had met was a frightening creature and he did not want to meet it again.

They had been living in their new home a week when another pair of otters arrived with a baby about Amikuk's age. They selected a spot close to the reef, and only a short distance from the kelp bed where Kahlan and his family fished and found shelter. It was natural for the two families to be neighborly. Before the sea otters had been driven to take refuge on the ocean, they had always lived together in communities upon land. There were many visits back and forth, and Amikuk played with his little neighbor. She was a lively little otter who swam as well as Amikuk. They played games of water tag and adventured among the seaweed and kelp, but neither of them was ever allowed to stray far from their mothers' protection.

The summer passed swiftly. At best it was never more than a brief time, with the sun warming the bleak shores and giving life to a few hardy plants. Amikuk grew and developed speed and grace. He could keep up with Kahlan and Bobry unless they exerted themselves, and he learned to dive to the most shallow submerged reef, a depth of some thirty feet. He could find sea urchins, but he was not able to break them open. He still had to depend upon his mother for this. His little friend was as capable as he, and they soon learned how to catch snails and crabs and other small crustaceans. They were able to break the shells of the crabs so they feasted most often in the shallow water where the seaweed grew. They suffered a few painful nips from the claws of the crabs before they learned how to handle them. Their mothers still nursed both of them and watched over them closely, but they were learning to fend for themselves.

Back at the hut near Black Reef, Peter worked hard gathering driftwood and helping his mother and father. Saan was happy because Kahgo seemed to have forgotten about otter hunting. Peter thought this might be because no otters had been sighted near the reef. For a while he made trips to the lookout ledge, hoping the otter family might return. He missed them, but he was glad they had escaped the hunters.

One day he and his father made a long trip down the coast seeking driftwood or a sea lion rookery from which they could secure a winter's supply of meat. They were shooting along through a rough sea when suddenly his father set his paddle and swerved the bidarkee. Peter was seated in the rear hole and did not at once see what had caused his father to change course. The bidarkee drifted and rose on a big wave. Kahgo pointed toward the east where a kelp bed spread inside the circle of a reef. Peter's gaze followed the pointing oar and he saw four otters floating near the kelp bed. With a smile, Kahgo turned the boat and sent it swiftly away from the reef. Peter was so intent upon the otters that he failed to stroke with his paddle. He realized that his father did not want to alarm the otters, and that made him worry. He was disturbed when

Kahgo did not halt to explore any of the coves for driftwood but paddled swiftly toward home. It meant that his father planned to hunt the otters or to tell Old Luca about them. And he was certain that one family was the one he had watched during the early summer.

At the reef, Amikuk and his family and friends were blissfully ignorant of any danger. Amikuk had met a band of thirty-two bachelor fur seals on their way south from their summer home. They had made the long journey from their home island, but they still had a thousand miles to travel. They selected the cove as a place to fish. They invaded the open water close to the kelp beds and were soon diving and leaping wildly. The otters took to the kelp bed and watched.

The young seals were a year old and about the same size and weight as Kahlan and Bobry. They were gray and black in color with lighter coloring on their shoulders and heads. They, like the otters, wore a robe valued by hunters, but for them protection had come in time to save them from extermination.

Amikuk stared at them out of his big eyes as they leaped and dived. They were master fishermen and the finest swimmers in the ocean. When they darted after a cod or a herring or a salmon, the fish had no chance to escape. They swam faster than the fastest fish, and they turned so sharply that no fish could dive or dart aside and escape them. For a half-hour they dived and fed, snapping up a fish and swallowing it after biting off and discarding the head, then dashing off after another. They had immense appetites and each devoured scores of fish before they stopped feeding and started playing games.

With amazing agility they rushed in and out among the rocks of the reef, playing tag through the breakers which smashed upon the boulders, racing in on the boiling currents and out again, grazing the ragged rocks but never touching them. When it seemed certain a big wave must smash them upon the rocks, they would flip backward and dart away. Tiring of defying the surf, they headed for open water. When they swam straight away, they stayed two or three feet underwater, and their dark bodies flashed along like shadows.

While they were fishing and playing games, the otters remained in the kelp bed watching. Amikuk would have liked to join the merry seals, but he was afraid to leave his mother's side. The seals swam in and out between the deep water and the reef. Suddenly a whale sounded close offshore, and a moment later the broad, black back appeared as the whale lifted its bulk out of the water. The whale was a humpback, and it was the biggest and most terrifying creature Amikuk had ever seen. He crowded against his mother's side, but she did not move or show alarm. Nor did the seals scatter in flight. Instead they darted toward the monster and circled around it. Some dived under the huge body, others sailed over it in flying leaps. Around and around, over and under the humpback leapt the seals. The whale swam lazily along, paying no attention to the sporting seals, and they followed it out to sea and down along the coast. They were still sporting around it when the whale vanished from sight.

The otters ventured out of the kelp bed, and Amikuk, with his small friend, swam to shallow water where they saw hundreds of fish heads floating among the seaweed. They paddled about catching snails and little crabs and shrimp. The four grown otters dived for sea urchins out in deep water.

After Peter and his father landed upon the big rock below the hut Kahgo hurried off to the village. Peter got into his kayak and paddled to a sheltered spot back of a big rock. As he had expected, five bidarkees soon appeared headed east along the shore. His father was in one of the boats with Old Luca. After they had passed, Peter followed them, keeping well back so that they would not see him.

As soon as the bidarkees had placed a headland between them and the village, they spread out in a single long line, keeping well abreast, at intervals of a few hundred feet between. The hunters paddled swiftly and silently over the water, each man peering into the vistas of churning waves ahead, eager to catch a glimpse of an otter's head. Fog swirled and twisted on the wind and the waves were white capped, but the sea was not one they considered rough. The fog allowed Peter to keep a half-mile behind the hunters without danger of being seen. He was sure that if his father saw him he would be sent home, and he wanted to see the hunt. He was hoping his friends would escape, though he knew there was nothing he could do to help them.

7: THE SURROUND

Amikuk was resting inside the kelp bed where the swell lifted and lowered his body gently. His mother and father were out in deep water diving for sea urchins along with their neighbors. Amikuk watched lazily, thinking that after a while he would swim out and join his little friend. She was sporting in the big waves. She would ride a wave as it started to build up and when its crest broke into white foam she would be perched on its very top ready to slide down into the trough and catch another ride.

Kahlan surfaced close to Bobry and lay on his back with a sea urchin clasped in his paws. He ripped it apart and started removing the meat. The neighbors surfaced and lay with their dinners on their broad breasts. Amikuk felt a stirring of hunger, but he was too lazy to do anything about it. He watched a large gull swoop down and land on the water close to his father. The gull stretched its neck and cocked its head sidewise as it moved closer to Kahlan. With a quick thrust of its beak it snatched at the meat spread on his breast. Kahlan gave a quick kick with one flipper, sending a shower of water over the gull. The gull flapped its wings and screamed as it backed away. Then its beak shot out again and nipped Kahlan sharply on the leg. With a wild jerk, he kicked out with both feet, sending his dinner flying through the air. The gull hastily snatched up as much meat as it could cram into its beak, and rose into the air.

Kahlan raised himself high out of the water and shook himself. He was very angry, but there was nothing he could do about it. Dropping back he examined the spot where the gull had nipped him. Finding he was not wounded, he turned back up and dived. Bobry and the other otters had watched with interest. The fierce expressions which were fixed on their faces did not allow them to show amusement, but they felt it. As soon as Kahlan dived, they went back to their dinners.

Amikuk's little friend had tired of riding the big waves, and she was swimming toward the kelp bed. He slid from among the fronds to meet her. His stomach had finally won against his laziness. He swam past her, heading toward the shallows with its matted seaweed. She followed him eagerly and they were abreast as they entered the waving mass of greens. They both made a great show of diving down into the shallow water for crabs and shrimp. The water was only four feet deep, and the bottom was muddied by the incoming waves so that they had to feel about with their paws to find their food. It was good training, similar to the blind hunting their parents did at greater depths upon the sub-merged reef.

Amikuk was searching the rocky bottom. He had stayed down about as long as he could. Finally he located a good-sized crab and seized it, pulling it from a crevice in the rocks. When he surfaced, he found his little friend already floating on her back, carefully peeling a shrimp. Amikuk avoided the reaching pinchers of the crab and broke it open. The little one put the shrimp into her mouth and swallowed it, then turned her head to watch him as he picked pink meat from the crab shell. She licked her lips hungrily as her round eyes followed his movements. Amikuk would not have been angry if she had helped herself to some of his crab meat. Instead, she started washing bits of shrimp husk from her furry breast. When she had finished, she dived.

The large crab furnished all of the meat Amikuk wanted. His friend surfaced with a cuttlefish clasped in her paws. She was very proud of her catch and played with it for a few minutes before starting to eat it. Amikuk tossed the empty crab shell out across the water. He soaped himself with a bit of kelp and rinsed away the lather. By the time he had finished washing, she had eaten all of the cuttlefish she wanted and tossed what was left aside. He lay watching her as she washed and cleaned her fur. Then they started back toward the kelp bed. They were tired, their big eyes blinking sleepily. Finding a thick bed of fronds they floated on their backs and drowsed.

Amikuk was wakened by strange sounds. The sounds were not the harsh crying of the gulls; they were sounds he had never heard before, high-pitched shouting and loud yelling. Though he had never heard the hunting cry of the island natives, the sounds filled him with fright. Lifting his head, he looked out over the water. He saw many boats, and each boat had two men in it armed with paddles and spears. The boats had formed a circle and the men were beating the water with their paddles as they shouted. He lowered his head but still watched. He saw nothing of his father or mother or the neighbors.

The hunters in their bidarkees had surprised the

The otters were down deep and swimming. They had been surprised and surrounded while they were down on the submerged reef. The hunters had waited until all of the otters dived before moving in. When they surfaced they were encircled. Without waiting to take a full breath, they had dived again as spears flashed and cut the water around them.

The hunters in four of the boats had hoisted paddles above spots where strings of bubbles floated upward. This told the others where the otters had dived. The hunter in the rear seat of a bidarkee handled the paddle while the man in front handled

otters while they were down on the submerged reef

the spears. The hunters were wildly excited because they had surrounded four otters, a fine stroke of luck. All of the boats had come to a halt waiting for furry heads to show again. They knew the otters could not stay down very long; they had not had time to fill their lungs with air.

Amikuk's friend was awake now and pressed fearfully against his side. His first impulse had been to swim out and find his mother. She had the same feeling, but the boats were such a terrifying sight that they could not move. They lay watching and listening to the shouting, eager for a glimpse of their parents.

The four otters within the circle of the boats broke water, exposing just their muzzles. But that was enough to bring wild shouts from the hunters, and a shower of spears struck the water while oars beat the surface. Again the otters dived, and again they could not catch a full breath. Though they were still strong and able to dive deep, they could not stay underwater very long. Once more they surfaced and were met with shouts and showering spears. The hunters were all eager to make a strike, but they did not worry when their spears missed their targets. They knew that in the end they would have targets that were not so active, and they would make their kills.

The grim struggle went on for an hour. Bobry was thinking only of her baby. She and the other mother worked their way toward the kelp bed while Kahlan and his friend kept to deeper water, trying to get out to sea and the haven of a fog bank. This divided the hunting party. Three boats stayed with Kahlan and his friend, two followed the mothers, trying to prevent them from reaching the kelp bed. Unluckily the otters had been feeding far out from the kelp beds, and this made escape more difficult for the mothers.

Bobry's friend was a weaker animal and she had

panicked more than Bobry. Failing to take in much air each time she surfaced, she had to break water more often. The hunters began to concentrate upon her. At last, interrupted respiration filled her with air and gasses until she could no longer force her body beneath the surface. A spear struck her, and as the two boats converged for the kill, Bobry made a last desperate effort to reach the kelp bed where her son lay. She managed to take a deep breath and lashed out with her flippers as she dived. Her body shot forward and suddenly she felt the pressure of broad fronds against her body. She lifted her head under cover of a broad frond and gasped for breath. Within a few minutes she had recovered enough to look for her son. She lifted the frond and peered about her. When she sighted Amikuk, she moved to his side. She was frantic because he and his friend were lying fully exposed watching the two boats out in the open water.

Amikuk recovered from his paralyzing fear when she thrust her muzzle against him. She caught hold of him and pulled him beneath the surface, then started pushing her way deeper into the kelp bed. Amikuk's little friend followed, keeping close to Bobry. Bobry looked back once and saw the hunters lift the carcass of the she-otter into one of the bidarkees. When the boats started moving toward the kelp bed, she struggled harder and worked her way deeper into the waving jungle.

Peter had watched the hunt and had become so interested that he had moved his kayak close to the three boats out in deep water. When he saw the hunters near the kelp bed pull a she-otter into their boat, he wondered if it was the mother he had once spared. He was shaken and there was a lump in his throat as he remembered the way that mother had looked up at him as he held her baby in his hand. He hoped the little one had escaped.

Out in deep water, Kahlan and his friend had separated. They had been fighting desperately for over an hour, and diving was becoming difficult. The brief moments when he was able to surface had shown Kahlan that there was a black fog bank ahead. The hunters saw the fog bank too and they pressed their attack. Kahlan knew that if he did not reach the fog bank soon he would not be able to escape. A spear had already cut a gash in his neck, penetrating the thick fur and opening a wound which was bleeding freely. His friend had turned west away from the fog bank. The hunters took advantage of this mistake. Two of the three boats followed the tiring otter, and a spear was ready when he at last failed to make a quick dive. Shouts of triumph rang out as the stricken otter was dragged aboard the bidarkee.

With only one boat to outwit, Kahlan struggled on toward the fog bank. This boat was manned by Kahgo and Old Luca. Kahgo handled the paddle while Old Luca sat ready with two spears. The realization that their prey might escape drove them to frantic efforts. Kahlan surfaced and Old Luca hurled his spear. It fell short by a foot, and Kahlan dived, urging his weary body toward the fog bank. He could stay under less than a minute now and his powerful flippers seemed to have lost all of their strength. He had to surface, and he rose slowly. His muzzle broke water, and he sucked in air. With the air came welcome wet mist, and his staring eyes looked up into a blanket of fog. He could hear the hunters shouting and the slap of Kahgo's paddle, but he could not see the bidarkee. He did not dive but swam sluggishly on through the fog, too weary to care greatly what happened or to pick any course except a blind flight away from the sounds coming through the fog. He swam on for a half-hour until the shouting faded away. The chance to breathe freely revived him; his strength had returned.

He could have kept on going out to sea and certain escape, but he turned his face toward shore and started back. He was thinking of Bobry and his son. He could not desert them even to save his own life. At the edge of the fog bank, he hesitated for a time, looking toward the kelp bed. The boats had gathered together for a council of war. The hunters were nervous because they were poaching. They could not be sure that a patrol boat would not pass that way or that someone on shore would not see them. The two otters they had taken would bring a big price when they delivered the skins to Ivan. Finally they decided to leave and turned their boats westward.

Kahlan watched the boats leave. When the fog had swallowed them, he went in search of Bobry and his son. He found them at the edge of the kelp bed. The orphan was with them, paddling about and whimpering for her mother. Kahlan was eager to be off before the hunters returned as he felt they would. This place was no longer safe, they must seek wilder, more desolate water. Bobry was willing to leave, but the orphan wanted to wait for her mother. The mother had always before returned to her. They swam about with her for a while, but finally Kahlan headed east. The orphan was afraid to stay alone so she followed them.

Kahlan led them out to the fog bank and then east along the shore. He kept on moving steadily until the little ones were so weary that Bobry called a halt and they rested. While the babies slept, Kahlan and Bobry remained awake and watchful. There was no thought of taking time to dive for food even though their meal had been interrupted and they were hungry. When Amikuk awakened, he nursed but the orphan had nothing to eat. She would nurse only on her mother's breast. She paddled about whimpering softly, not knowing what to do.

As they moved on, she swam more slowly. Kahlan set his pace so that she did not drop behind, and they did not abandon her. The miles slipped behind them and finally they heard the roar of sea lions coming out of the fog. Rocky headlands appeared and a large bay opened up before them. They could see inviting kelp beds and a reef offshore. Bobry knew the little ones needed rest, and the kelp bed looked so safe and inviting that she headed toward it. Kahlan would have preferred to keep on moving, but he followed her.

The kelp bed offered a welcome refuge. The otters worked their way deep into the tangled fronds.

They were so weary that they did not think of food. All they wanted was to rest and sleep. The roaring of the sea lions rose above the boom of the surf, but it did not disturb their slumber.

8 : SEA LIONS

For days after the hunt, Peter watched and waited. He had returned from the hunt without being seen, and he did not tell his father that he had watched the surround. Peter noticed that his father went to the village regularly, but that he never returned with more than the meager supplies he usually bought. This led Peter to believe his father had gotten none of the wealth from the otter pelts, and it made him feel better.

If his mother guessed there had been a hunt she never mentioned it, nor did she complain that she could not have a new dress for winter. He could not understand why he felt sorry about the hunt. Hunters had to kill to secure meat and to get money to buy sugar and tea and cloth; fish had to be killed and seals and sea lions and foxes. But somehow the otter family seemed different. He had known them so well and watched them so much.

One morning his father said they would go to the cliffs and net little auks so that Saan could make a bird pie. Peter was pleased. Netting auks was great sport and always resulted in a feast. His mother brightened at once and laughed as Peter got the long pole and the net from the pegs on the outside wall of the hut.

"We will have a good pie," she said.

"And I will eat like the killer whale," Peter answered.

Kahgo carried the pole and the net while Peter carried a willow basket to gather eggs and to carry the auks they would catch. They climbed up over the rocky ground to the cliff base. The cliffs overlooking the ocean swarmed with nesting birds. A big flock of red-legged turnstones had paused to rest on their way north to the seal islands, where they would spend the summer feasting upon the swarms of flies and gnats which followed the seal herds. There were thousands of gulls upon the cliffs and in the air. Peter liked to watch the great burgomaster gulls as they soared high overhead in endless sweeps. But he was interested in the eggs of the arries and the lupus more than in the eggs of the gulls. The eggs of the gulls were too strong in flavor to be relished except in an omelette where they could be mixed with savory roots.

"We will gather the eggs first," his father said as they stood looking up at the ledges crowded with birds.

Having given this order, Kahgo sat down and lighted his pipe. Peter's nimble legs were better suited to clambering along the narrow shelf. He climbed up to the first shelf and the birds launched into hasty flight, screaming in alarm. He had no trouble in finding eggs. The arries and the lupus laid their eggs in any crevice or depression in the bare cliff wall. They made no nests and were careful only to place the eggs where they would not roll off the shelf. The eggs of the arries were about the same size as hens' eggs and were white in color. They were delicious boiled or fried in oil. The lupus's eggs were about the size of a goose egg, and they were gaily colored. Peter piled the eggs into his basket until it was half full.

When he climbed down and set the basket at his father's feet, Kahgo picked out some of the eggs and tossed them aside. He could tell which eggs were fresh and discarded those that had started to hatch or were old and stale.

"How can you tell?" Peter asked.

"By the color and the feel," his father answered.

After the eggs were sorted, they climbed to the top of the cliff. The wind was gusty. It pulled at them and buffeted them. They had to plant their feet firmly to keep from being swept away. There was something about the wind which added to the excitement of the hunt.

Kahgo fastened the closely meshed net to the end of the pole. The net was held open by a loop of bent willow. Kahgo braced his feet firmly as he stood up. Peter crouched at his feet beside the basket. Overhead swarms of little auks swept low over the cliff. Kahgo lifted the net as a flock swept toward him. He gave it a quick sweep and four auks flew into it. Quickly he lowered the net and reached inside it. He dispatched each auk with a pinch at the back of its neck, then handed the birds to Peter.

The auks were bright and fearless birds with round and fat bodies. Peter's mouth watered as he thought of the big pie his mother would make. His father kept on netting auks until the basket was full. When he finally removed the net from the pole he knelt down beside Peter.

"Can you carry so much?" he asked.

"I can carry the basket," Peter answered. He was sure he could manage, but he would have to be careful until he was over the rim and down on the lee side of the cliff. The wind tugged and twisted at the basket as though trying to wrench it from his grasp.

They moved carefully and reached the base of the cliff without a mishap. Peter wanted to run ahead with the basket to show his mother what a fine catch they had made, but his father walked without haste so he restrained himself. Saan met them on the path above the hut and took the basket from Peter. She exclaimed delightedly over the auks and the fresh eggs. When they reached the hut, Kahgo seated himself on a rock to smoke while Peter helped his mother pluck the auks and get them ready for the big baking dish.

It was a wonderful meal. Peter ate so much auk pie that he wasn't sure he'd be able to get up from the box where he sat. The big meal made him sleepy and he had to nod his head and blink his eyes to keep awake. His father was in a very good humor. He smiled at Peter as he cracked a boiled egg.

"If you will scout along the coast in your kayak for sea lions we will make a drive for winter meat and for oil."

Peter's eyes popped open at once. "I will scout tomorrow," he said. He was glad his father was going to hunt the big ones. He knew his mother had been worried because Kahgo and the hunters at the village had not gone out after sea lions. Isolated villages and lone hunters must stay with the old ways and not depend so much upon the trading post, she felt.

The new home of the otters was separated from the rookery of the sea lions by a curving backbone of rocks which extended out from the shore. The sea lions had their own bay where they swam and fished. At high tide there were many waterways between the rocks, but at low tide the barrier made a tight fence.

To Amikuk the sea lion rookery was a strange and terrible place. He spent many hours gazing at the rocks where the big fellows rested after fishing or frolicking in the deep water at the foot of their cliffs. By swimming close to the reef, he could see everything that went on in the rookery.

The bull sea lions were six feet in height when sitting up on a rock. They measured ten feet in length, with a girth of nine feet around the chest and shoulders, and their heavy bass voices drowned out the boom of the surf that thundered on the rocks below the rookery. Their coats were a rich golden rufous in color. The faces of the old bulls were fierce even in repose. Their small eyes showed clearly, and their long tusks gleamed white against black tongues. The females were smaller and milder-looking, and they seldom bellowed.

The first time Amikuk watched the sea lions, he witnessed a fight between two surly old bulls. While he was watching, the two bulls started quarreling. After bellowing savagely at each other for some minutes, they started moving slowly together. They averted their faces as though they could not stand the sight of each other even though they must fight. Their heads darted back and forth like striking snakes. Each was waiting for an unguarded moment when he could strike. The moment came, and one bull struck, sinking his fangs into the neck of his opponent and clenching his powerful jaws. A wild struggle followed until the victim literally tore himself loose from the other's fangs, leaving a gaping wound. Fired by pain and rage, the wounded bull struck back, and hair and blood flew in every direction. The rocks upon which they struggled were red with their blood.

Amikuk wanted to dash to his mother, but the sight of the struggling bulls held him. They fought savagely, intent upon destroying each other, until one of them was hurled off the rocks and plunged into the bay. He sank with a great splash but arose at once and lifted himself out of the water. Bellowing his defiance, he swam slowly away from the shore, unwilling or unable to climb back upon the rocks. The victorious bull fanned himself with a flipper and roared a defiant battle cry. He did not lick his wounds but sat glaring down at the bay, ignoring the open slashes on his neck and shoulders.

The defeated bull swam toward the flat rocks behind which Amikuk was floating. His head lifted out of the water and his jaws worked. Amikuk whirled and fled to his mother. With the monster less than a hundred feet away, he thought of nothing but retreat. He did not remember that a rocky barrier separated him from the huge beast. Reaching Bobry's side, he snuggled close to her. She wasn't excited about the sea lions, and his father ignored them as long as they stayed beyond the rock barrier. They both knew that the sea lions could not catch them unless the sea lions surprised them asleep in open water. But they were careful to avoid the fishing grounds of the monsters; they knew the big ones would eagerly make a meal of a sea otter, given the chance to catch one napping. The way his father and mother acted toward the big fellows reassured Amikuk, and he soon left his mother's side to play in the waves.

He tried to get the orphan to play with him, but she would not follow him. Now that her mother was gone, she did not seem able to seek small creatures among the seaweed or to help herself in any way. She lay beside the kelp bed, her eyes fixed hopefully on the open sea. Although she was desperately hungry, her longing for her mother was greater than the gnawing pangs in her stomach. Amikuk coaxed her but she would not come with him. Finally he swam away to hunt sails and crabs in the shallow water near shore. As he hunted he kept an eye on the sea lion rookery and on the bay below it where many heads were bobbing as the big ones fished and played.

Later that day, an extra heavy tide came in and the barrier was almost completely submerged. Kahlan became uneasy, and he moved his family closer to the kelp beds. The tangled jungle was not affected by the tide. It rode the high water unchanged except that it seemed more restless as it churned up and down. There was never a time when there were no sea lions in the water, and some of them might wander out of the deep bay and into the otter's fishing ground. There was always a steady procession of sea lions going down to the bay and another procession climbing out and hauling themselves up over the black rocks. The huge beasts showed remarkable agility in clambering up over the slippery rocks, and they were masterful swimmers.

AMIKUK

Amikuk spent most of his time during the next few days playing near the kelp bed or floating close to the reef were he could see the sea lions. He had ceased trying to get the orphan to go adventuring with him and went alone. His mother allowed him to stray farther from her side because he was fast becoming a strong swimmer. He always sought the shallow water to hunt for crabs and shrimp and then floated beside the reef, watching the sea lions as they fished or sported. The sea lions were always happiest when the surf was running strong and wild and when a hurricane wind was blowing. They delighted in riding the crest of each dissolving breaker up to the moment when it smashed upon the rocks in a spume of white foam. At that moment they would disappear beneath the foaming water to reappear upon the crest of the next angry billow. When swimming, they would lift their heads above water for a deep breath of air, then dart forward a few feet beneath the surface. When lazing or playing, they moved in a leisurely fashion, but if a killer whale's tall fin was sighted, they were off at terrific speed. They had as great a dread of the killers as the otters had. Big and bulky as they were, these whales were able to take almost any fish or sea animal they sighted.

SEA LIONS

Soon Amikuk began to feel that the sea lions were not dangerous but were really his friends. He still had an important lesson to learn. One day while Bobry and Kahlan were diving far out in deep water, he slipped through the barrier and swam into the bay where the big fellows fished. He paddled about eagerly, staring at the huge animals as they dived and leaped.

He became so interested in a pair of young sea lions that he ventured well out into the bay. Lifting his head high, he watched them race around and around in a game of water tag. This was a game he often played with his father and mother and he wanted very much to join them, but he wasn't quite sure they would welcome him. Suddenly a big bull rose out of the water not twenty feet from him. The monster weighed over fifteen hundred pounds, and his ugly face was grizzled with a stiff beard of quill-like hairs. His small eyes glared fiercely, his tusks gleamed white against his black tongue and lips. He shook himself as he rose high on a wave and rumbled deep in his throat. He was surprised to see so fine a morsel of food before him and he lost no time in plunging toward Amikuk.

The little otter darted to one side and dived. He went down as deep as he could and worked his flippers with all of his strength. Twisting and ducking, he looked back. The big bull was gaining upon him. This was his first real test, and Amikuk did his best, which was fast enough to keep him ahead of the gaping jaws for a few seconds. He shot upward and broke water in a long leap. As he left the water, the bull shot under him. Amikuk's maneuver surprised the sea lion and threw him off balance. He had to make a sharp turn and his bulky body did not respond as quickly as Amikuk's slender form. The brief respite gave Amikuk a chance to dash closer to the barrier. He swam blindly, not knowing where the narrow opening through which he had come was located. The big bull quickly made his turn and gave chase. His speed was far greater than Amikuk's, but the little otter had gained a lead. In a last desperate spurt, he shot toward the rocks and saw an opening big enough for his body to pass through. He leapt into the opening just as the tusks of the bull snapped at his tail. The big fellow could not follow; his girth was too great to squeeze between the rocks. He rose out of the water and bellowed furiously at being cheated out of a choice meal. Amikuk had surfaced, but when the bull roared he dived again, as deep as he could.

Amikuk did not stop his flight until he reached

his mother's side. He snuggled close against her, and she sensed his fright. She lifted him to her broad breast and let him share the sea urchin she was eating. As he nibbled bits of meat, he kept watching the barrier separating him from the sea lions' bay. He was expecting to see the old bull come clambering over the rocks, and he wanted to be ready to warn his mother. The bull did not appear, and finally Amikuk let his mother deposit him on the kelp bed so that she could finish her diving.

The day after the sea lion adventure, while Amikuk and his father and mother were playing tag, the orphan left the kelp bed and swam toward open water. She moved past the family, and they stopped frolicking to watch her. They did not try to call her back, and she never looked their way. She was seeking the cove where she had left her mother. She stroked slowly, her body filled with a dragging weariness. She was not sure of her directions and was soon swimming south, heading out into the vast Pacific Ocean. A gull swept low over her and cried harshly as though to warn her. A big china shark rolled over lazily and watched her. The dull-witted killer mistook her for a fur seal and sank down into the shadowy depths. She passed on out of the swirling mists which shrouded the coast of the island chain. At intervals she called for her mother, and she kept looking hopefully ahead as she rode the crest of each wave. She kept on swimming through the night, and through the next day, until weariness began to claim her, and she lay on her back drifting with the wind. She was barely aware of the roaring storm which swept over her and drew her down into the green shadow-filled world and on to the blackness below.

For a day or so, Amikuk missed the orphan, but he soon forgot all about her. He no longer ventured past the rock barrier, but he was still interested in the sea lions, and watched them every day. He was now catching more than half of the food he needed, and that made him more independent of Bobry. But he would have suffered the same fate as the little orphan if he had lost his mother. He still needed her and depended upon her. Months would pass before he would be able to fend for himself.

When the tide was full, the family had to be watchful for bull sea lions. The big fellows roved far and were always looking for otters as well as fish. Amikuk was learning that the kelp beds were the safest refuge. The sea lions would not penetrate the interlacing jungle nor would the killer whale nor the shark. The kelp beds were to the otter what the briar patch is to the gray fox and the cottontail rabbit. By living near such a jungle, the family could quickly take refuge. Out in open water, they depended upon sharp eyes and keen noses to warn them of danger and give them time to dive before they were sighted.

9 : OLD FRIENDS

Peter set out in his kayak early in the morning. He planned to spend the entire day scouting the coast for sea lions. Peter was worried about his father. A government man had caught Ivan, the trader, with two otter pelts in his possession, and Peter was sure they were the two pelts that the village hunters had taken. His father and the other hunters would be in trouble if Ivan told the government man the names of the men who had killed the otters. Peter did not think his father had taken any of the money, but Kahgo was upset. Peter knew he was trying to keep Saan from noticing how worried he was.

The sea was running moderately rough, but there was only a high fog, which did not obscure the shore rocks and the cliffs. Peter paddled east along the coast. He had brought along boiled eggs and dried fish for his noon meal, and he had his spear with him though he did not expect to use it. His worries left him as he sent the kayak skimming over the water. This was summertime and every Aleut was happy during the brief weeks of bounty. Swarms of birds flew overhead, swirling out to sea or back to the cliffs and the green slopes. It seemed hardly possible that soon the cliffs and the sky would be deserted, the birds gone. But Peter knew that they would leave when winter storms lashed the coast with sleet and snow.

It was almost noon when he heard the bellowing of the bulls on the sea lion rookery. He did not approach close enough for them to see him but beached the kayak in a little cove back of a big rock. He would do his scouting from there on foot. He took his lunch and his spear and climbed to the top of a ridge. He followed the ridge to a point from which he could look down upon the shore rocks, unnoticed by the sea lions.

He lay on his stomach and looked over the edge of a rim. He knew what he must look for and be able to describe to his father and Old Luca. First he watched the big fellows as they moved back and forth between the bay and the rocks. This was a large rookery and a drive would capture a fine herd. If the hunters from the village helped, a half-dozen men might capture as many as fifty or more sea lions. After checking the number of animals, Peter gave his attention to the coast. There was a narrow stretch of surf-beaten beach and a long slope above the big rocks where the sea lions hauled themselves out of the bay. What would have appeared to be an impossible feat to anyone but an Aleut seemed quite reasonable to Peter. A few men could make an assault upon this rookery. Satisfied that the drive could be made, Peter gave his attention to the bay and the barrier which flanked it. His eyes moved beyond the reef and suddenly he felt a thrill of excitement pass through him.

He sat up and stared down at the kelp bed beyond the barrier. Three sea otters were playing tag close to the waving kelp. He strained his eyes trying to see if the otters were his old friends. The little one was much larger than the baby he had caught, but that was only natural. They were too far away for him to be certain, but he had a feeling they were the same family. He was glad they had escaped from the hunters.

To make sure they were his friends he worked his way around the rookery and down to the reef. He crawled from rock to rock until he was as far out on the reef as he could possibly get without being seen by the otters. Crouching behind a rock, he watched them for a long time. Before he left he was sure they were his friends.

Finding the otters near the rookery gave Peter a problem. If he led the hunters to the sea lion rookery they might see the otters and want to hunt them. He knew he should tell about the rookery. His family and the villagers needed oil and meat for winter, and besides it was likely that scouts from the village would find the sea lions. By the time he had worked his way back to where he had beached the kayak he had made up his mind. He would tell his father about the rookery. He ate his lunch and slid the kayak into the water. Once headed for home, he sent the little craft skimming ahead swiftly.

The otters had never suspected that they were being watched by a human being. When the game of tag ended they swam out to deep water where Bobry and Kahlan started diving for food. When his mother dived, Amikuk turned over and followed her down. The submerged reef was sixty feet down, much deeper than the twenty- and thirty-foot dives he had made before. He thrust his body down through the water with powerful strokes, trying to keep up with his mother. Suddenly he lost sight of her, and darkness engulfed him. But he kept on stroking strongly.

Panic tugged inside him as the darkness closed in around him. He reached down with his paws, hoping to find bottom. The water seemed to be pressing upon him as though bent upon squeezing him. He was not bothered by lack of air but the strange world around him was frightening. Monsters might be lurking close by that he could not see. He was not aware of a single fish though the upper waters had been teeming with them. Then his paws found rocky bottom, and he started frantically feeling about for a sea urchin. He located a spiny shell and tugged at it. It pulled free of the rock, and he twisted about for a fast return to the surface. He shot upward as fast as his flippers would send him. Grayness showed above him, then pale green and suddenly he was flashing through a school of herring, sending them scattering in all directions. He burst out of the water clutching the sea urchin. His father and mother floated a few yards away. They were calmly tearing apart their prizes. Bobry turned her head and watched her son with interest.

Amikuk struggled with the tough shell. He tugged at it with all of his strength. Now that he had made a deep dive and secured a sea urchin, he wanted to break the shell himself. He knew how it was done, having watched his mother many times. But the shell refused to be torn apart. Bobry made a lazy movement and slid to his side. She took his catch and tore it apart. Eagerly Amikuk reached for the half shells and placed them upon his breast. He felt very proud of himself as he lay beside his mother sucking the sweet meat out of the shell. When he finished one half, he tossed the shell as far as he could throw it. Bobry and Kahlan were proud of their son, but there was no way they could let him know.

Amikuk carefully followed the ritual observed by his parents. He soaped and washed himself thoroughly before diving again. His second dive ended in failure. His mother shared her second catch with him. But this did not satisfy him, and he dived again and again until he secured his second sea urchin. Again Bobry had to tear it apart for him, but he was happy, and he was very weary, ready for a nap.

The family floated out over deep water and lazed. Their stomachs were full, and they were content to let the waves lift them and lower them like children in a swing. Suddenly Kahlan sounded an alarm and dived. Amikuk raised his head and looked across the water before he followed his mother in a dive. He saw a kayak approaching manned by a small hunter who was stroking swiftly. The hunter was shouting and splashing loudly with his paddle. Amikuk doubled up and dived after his mother. He could see her streaking along four feet under the surface, heading toward the kelp bed. He followed her into the tangle of fronds, and they worked their way deep into the bed where they found Kahlan.

When they halted, Amikuk poked his head up under a frond and peered toward open water. The kayak had halted and was bobbing up and down close to the floating kelp. After a long wait, it turned and made off toward the open sea. The otters watched until the kayak and the small hunter disappeared into a fog bank.

Kahlan wanted to be off at once, but Bobry would not leave the kelp bed. She intended to wait until darkness settled. She knew they could not stay after being seen by a hunter, but she was afraid to leave the protection of the kelp jungle. She knew what would happen if Amikuk was caught in open water. Kahlan finally stopped coaxing, and they lay waiting for darkness.

Before night settled upon them a storm broke. It was a gale of hurricane force which built up huge waves and lashed the sea into a churning inferno.

The storm roused the sea lions to defiant bellowing and filled the otters with wild excitement, but it also kept them within the protecting kelp bed where they lay secure from the lashing wind and the pounding waves and the icy sleet which hissed and battered upon them.

The storm lashed the coast for three days, and during that time the otters did not venture out into open water to dive for food. They caught a few snails and some crustaceans and several befuddled surface fish, but this was lean fare for creatures with big appetites. Amikuk fared best because his mother nursed him, but Kahlan and Bobry grew gaunt.

When the storm broke, Kahlan forgot about running away. He and Bobry hurried out to deep water and Amikuk followed them. The cove was still very rough, but Amikuk dived along with his parents and was able to capture two sea urchins, which his mother opened for him. The family fed hugely and did not stop diving until they could eat no more. After they had satisfied their hunger, they returned to the kelp bed and hid themselves. Bobry and Amikuk went to sleep at once. Kahlan remained on watch for a half-hour before he took a nap.

Peter had given his father a complete description of the sea lion rookery without mentioning the otters. He was sure he had frightened them away, so there was no need to mention them. Kahgo was eager to organize a drive, but he hesitated about going to the village for fear the government man might be there. In the end he went and talked to Old Luca. When he returned to the hut, he brought news that a drive would be made. Six hunters would join him and Peter. Old Luca had picked the hunters, but it was understood that everyone in the village would share the meat and oil and skins. Preparations got underway at once. Saan helped get ready the needed material. She brought out a faded pink parasol, a tin horn which had been given to Peter by a missionary, and some cloth which she tore into strips. Peter knotted seal hide strips into a long rope while Kahgo checked the bidarkee and saw that the spears were ready. They had everything loaded and were waiting at the landing when the three bidarkees from the village appeared.

Saan had packed a basket of food which was tucked away inside the skin boat. Peter and his father laced themselves into their places and shoved off to meet their friends. They were greeted with eager shouts, and the four bidarkees danced away across the water with Peter and his father leading the procession.

The distance to the rookery was ten miles overland and a little farther by water because of the curving coast line. The swift bidarkees made the trip in two hours. Peter led them into the same cove where he had beached his kayak, and they hauled their boats up out of reach of high tide. Before they climbed up on the ledge for a look at the rookery, they built a shelter of skins which would form a windbreak. They set their baskets of food and their equipment close to the shelter wall.

Before climbing the ridge, the hunters ate a meal out of their baskets. They sat close to the windbreak and talked in low voices. These hunters were not big men. Kahgo, the tallest man among them, stood only five feet five inches in height. Old Luca, a veteran hunter with a wrinkled, leathery face, was only four feet two inches tall, two inches less than Peter's height. He was a gnomelike little man with long arms and powerful shoulders. The hunters all wore their black hair long, and their faces were broad with high cheek bones, their noses small and flat, and their eyes slanted a little. Living so much in a cramped bidarkee had given them sprung knees, but the constant wielding of paddles had developed their arms and shoulders. They were a good-natured group, quick to laugh, loving to talk when not hunting. Their village was off the main courses of travel and so isolated that they lived much as their ancestors had lived for hundreds of years.

The meal was finished quickly because the hunters were eager to get on with their plans. Peter led them up to the top of the ridge and along it to the lookout point where he had watched the rookery. They crawled to the edge of the rim and looked down. Peter could tell by the expressions on their faces that they were much pleased by what they saw. He could feel the excitement that was building up in them. While the hunters were intent upon the sea lions and the rookery, Peter scanned the water beyond the reef. His pulses quickened when he saw three heads bobbing far out near the kelp beds. His plan to frighten the otter family away had failed. At any moment the sharp eyes of one of the hunters might spot his friends.

But the hunters were so absorbed with the sea lions that they wasted no time in scanning the water beyond the bay. They were interested in the narrow beach and in the slope above the rookery as much as they were interested in the big animals. They checked the procession of sea lions going and coming from the bay and estimated their numbers.

116

They lay there, eight puny humans, and planned an assault upon the angry-looking beasts below, many of which weighed more than fifteen hundred pounds and whose bellowing rose above the boom of the surf. After an hour of watching, they slipped down the face of the cliff to their camp. Peter was glad none of them had mentioned the otters.

The men sat on the rocks sheltered from the wind by the skins they had erected. If the night was right, they could proceed at once. The weather seemed favorable but it might not hold that way. Peter returned to the ridge above and lay watching the otter family. There was no way he could warn them now. All he could hope for was that no one had seen them but himself. He stayed late on the ridge and when he reached camp, the men were stirring, getting everything ready for the drive. As he stood watching he was startled to hear Old Luca say:

"Out beyond the reef, there are three otters."

The hunters turned their faces toward him and several of the men frowned. Kahgo shook his head. "We cannot sell the skins. It is foolish to think of taking them."

"We can keep them and sell them when the chance comes. Ivan was taken away, but we have the money he gave us," Old Luca said.

"When we spend the money, the government man will ask where we got it," Kahgo said. "That is why I will not take any of it."

"I think not," Old Luca said. "I will hunt the otters after the drive is made."

Kahgo shrugged his shoulders. "I will not hunt them," he said.

Looking from face to face, Peter knew that Old Luca would have help in killing the otters. He had picked men who had been with him when the other otters were taken. Peter wanted to speak out but knew this would not be proper as he was only a boy. This was a matter for the men to handle. He sat down on a rock and stared gloomily at the tin horn he was to carry.

Night came and there was a moon, partially obscured by drifting clouds. It was a fine night for a drive, and the hunters hastily gathered up the things they would need. Kahgo carried the pink parasol, Peter tucked the tin horn under his arm. There was a short discussion so that the plans would be understood by all. Old Luca took the lead, and they started moving along the shore on foot keeping close to the water's edge.

The tide was out, exposing a strip of hard sand. When they neared the rookery, the hunters got down on their hands and knees and crawled on all fours. They moved slowly between the sleeping herd and the ocean. The sea lion sentries could not be sure in the uncertain light that the human forms were not seals. Peter crept close behind his father. He knew that all of the giant bulls lying with their faces to the bay would escape. No power could stop a thousand-pound bull once he headed toward the water. Each hunter had to be alert to keep from being smashed in the first moments of excitement. He peered over Kahgo's back at the looming forms above him and wondered if the bull directly above him was facing the bay.

Old Luca halted, and the other hunters stopped. Muscles were taut as they waited for the order to attack. Kahgo opened the parasol and Peter got his tin horn to his lips. He was still watching the huge black shape close above him.

"Ready!" Old Luca shouted as he leaped to his feet.

Instantly the night was filled with wild shouts, beating of sticks, the shrill squawking of Peter's horn, and the rattle of tin plates the hunters had brought with them. A terrific bellow arose from the throats of the sea lions. And as they bellowed, every animal lunged forward. Those facing the bay lunged that way, those facing up the slope lunged in that direction, moving at amazing speed, bal-

Instantly the night was filled with shouts, beating of stick

ancing awkwardly, their heavy necks swinging as a lever, to and fro with every forward hitch of their hind flippers.

Before Peter realized it, the big bull above him was charging down upon him. He turned to dive aside but caught his foot on a projecting rock and sprawled face down. He felt a jarring impact which sent him rolling over and over. When he scrambled to his feet, the big bull was gone, and the hunters were well above him, pursuing the floundering sea lions. He felt his arms and legs and decided he was not hurt. A few minutes search located his horn, but it was useless; the bull had smashed it flat. Tossing it aside, he ran up the slope as fast as he could.

rattle of tin plates, and the squawking of Peter's horn.

The hunters were uttering horrible noises as they danced and leaped behind the terrified animals. They brandished sticks and beat on the tin plates. The huge beasts were wild with fright and floundered on, not caring in what direction they were headed. The rout did not last very long because the sea lions were not able to travel far on land without rest. Soon they fell panting and gasping upon the rocks, helpless in spite of their bulk and powerful muscles and at the mercy of their captors. The hunters could have dispatched all of the sixty or more animals, but they had no desire to drag hides and meat down to the bidarkees and then paddle weary miles to the village. Such an undertaking would have taken many trips and much hard work. As soon as the sea lions regained their breath, the hunters rudely roused them and drove them on. It would take six days and nights to cover the ten miles to the village, but it was the best way.

The party divided, half of them returning to the bidarkees to pack up and take the boats back, the other half remaining to drive the herd. Peter wanted to help drive, and his father was willing.

The men kept the herd moving all night, with brief rests at intervals. Toward morning they made a corral so that they, themselves, could stop and get some rest. The corral was a simple enclosure, and looked absurd as a stockade which would restrain sixty huge beasts. The sea lions were huddled into a group, and the men drove stakes into the ground, forming a circle around the pod. Thong ropes were stretched between the stakes, and strips of cloth tied to the ropes. The strips flapped in the wind in a manner terrifying to the sea lions. One man was left to watch while the others slept. The big fellows would remain huddled together for several hours, and not one would attempt to break through the flimsy barrier. Peter closed the parasol Kahgo had given him and lay down on the rocky ground. He needed no soft bed to bring sleep.

But before he closed his eyes, Peter spent some

time worrying about the otters. Old Luca had stayed behind to bring back one of the bidarkees. He might talk the other men into hunting the otters, though Peter did not think his father would join the hunt. But even so big a worry could not keep Peter awake very long. He was soon snoring soundly.

10 : ISLAND HOME

$\mathbf{A}$mikuk awakened to find his mother shaking him. The moment he opened his eyes and cried out, she pulled him from the frond bed where he had been sleeping and spilled him into the water. He paddled sleepily for a minute or so before he heard the strange sounds coming from the rocky shore where the sea lions lived. The sounds reminded him of something which frightened him. He dived to his mother's side and stayed close to her. His father was waiting just out from the kelp bed. For a little while, the three otters lay looking toward the rookery and listening.

The clouds swept away from the moon for a brief space, and they were able to see the hunters driving the sea lions up the slope. The sight so frightened Kahlan and Bobry that they turned and fled. Bobry swam beside Amikuk and urged him to his top speed. He needed no urging to make him swim as fast as he could. The sight of the hunters leaping and dancing while the sea lions charged wildly up over the rocks was enough to make him strain every muscle.

There was no need for Bobry to drag or carry her son. He had developed into a sturdy swimmer. Kahlan led them out of the cove into open water. He set his course away from the coast, trusting the open sea. When he was far out, he shifted directions and faced west. They swam on through the night, pausing only to let Amikuk rest and nurse. When gray dawn lighted the expanse of ocean around them Bobry started scanning the horizon for a sheltered cove and a kelp bed. She saw nothing but sea and sky. Even from the crest of the highest wave, she could not see a shore line in any direction.

Kahlan was beginning to mistrust the mainland. The hunters he feared frequented the shore; they were land animals. So he turned away from the mainland, seeking a more secluded and if possible a more desolate spot. He found nothing but open water that day and knew he must seek shallow water or they would starve. Turning toward the main island chain again, he swam on, and on the second day they sighted a low-lying island.

The island was small with spots of sand beach

between rocky outcroppings. Surf pounded the rocks and hurled spray high into the air. The interior of the island was low and rolling with numerous fresh-water ponds dotting green valleys. The entire coast circuit was less than ten miles. There were no trees on the island, but there was moss and grass. Kahlan led them around the island, keeping well out from shore. The only living things to be seen were multitudes of ducks and geese swimming on the fresh-water ponds.

They had arrived during low tide. Southward of the island, a chain of rocky, barren islets extended out into the ocean. These islets and the numerous reefs connecting them would be submerged during storms and high water. On the lee sides of the reefs, large kelp beds lay, rising and falling in the swell. There were no high cliffs to break the wind so that the waters around the island were turbulent most of the time. Kahlan liked the island. Here were reefs and kelp beds for protection against killers from the sea, and here no hunters in boats could approach without being seen. Bobry liked the kelp beds, and Amikuk was eager to stop any place where he could dive for food and find a calm bed of kelp to sleep upon.

They moved in close to the south shore and soon all three were diving for sea urchins. A bit of exploring by Kahlan and Bobry located a submerged reef in forty feet of water. When Amikuk saw his father and mother surface with food in their paws, he swam swiftly to the spot and dived. He located the reef and secured a sea urchin. Floating on his back, he gripped the shell and pulled hard. Bobry moved toward him to crack the shell for him, but, to his and to her surprise, he ripped it open by his own efforts. He was so proud of what he had done that he forgot he was hungry and paddled about showing off before his parents.

Amikuk was nearing the time when he would be able to care for himself and would not need his mother's help and guidance. He asserted his independence by swimming off by himself and exploring other kelp beds along the shore. Bobry no longer worried when she did not know where he was. She gave more of her time to Kahlan, staying closer to him and playing with him as much as she played with Amikuk.

The first real sign of winter came when the flocks of ducks and geese arose from the ponds and flew southward. The ducks swirled away, with the teals moving fast and in compact formation while the slower mallards and spoonbills circled into the upper air before leaving. The geese took their V-shaped formations and followed their leaders. Amikuk listened to their honking long after they had vanished into the misty sky. The sound filled him with a strange uneasiness. He sensed that a change in his way of life was coming. His mother and father understood and did not mind the loneliness which settled upon the island. Now the only living things, aside from the dwellers of the underwater world, were the three sea otters. Kahlan was well pleased with the solitude. He had his family and an abundance of food; this was all he desired.

The first bitter storms roared down out of the north with a fury that lashed even the kelp beds to a frenzy. It captured gulls and carried them along with it. Even their sturdy wings could not save them; they could neither escape from the grip of the wind nor could they guide their flight. Like swirling leaves they rode the storm, knowing that somewhere to the south it would spend its fury and release them.

The three otters clung to the kelp bed close inshore. They buried their heads in heaps of seaweed above the wash of the surf where they were free from the flying spray and beating waves. This was as near to a landing as Kahlan would make. They huddled close together for three days while the storm raged and black fog made day almost as dark as night. Sleet and snow hissed over them and piled drifts on the lee sides of the island's boulders.

At last the storm broke and the hungry otters swam out to deep water to dive for food. They feasted until their bellies were round and tight; then they drowsed, looking up into the wintry sky. The air was brittle and cold after the storm, but this did not bother the otters, wrapped as they were in thick robes that defied the cold and the water.

Amikuk floated close to a kelp bed. He reached out lazily and pulled a frond from the mass beside him. Wadding it into a ball he tossed it into the air and caught it before it struck the water. Without exerting himself, he played ball for a half hour, then fell asleep. His mother and father were napping, relaxed after the long siege of wind and snow. A current caught him and pulled him away from the kelp bed. It carried him out toward deep water. Amikuk was now sound asleep, and the current did not rouse him. Kahlan and Bobry did not sleep so soundly; when the current tugged at them, they lazily stroked with a flipper.

Amikuk was roused from slumber by a jarring blow. The instant his eyes popped open, he turned over and dived. He had not seen the enemy that had struck him; the quick flip and the dive were instinctive. Before the water closed over him he gave one wild cry for his mother. Fear made him stroke as powerfully as he could, but his flippers did not send him darting downward as they should; his body angled off sluggishly to one side. His back felt numb but there was no pain. He circled slowly, only a few feet under the surface.

Then he saw the enemy that had struck him. A shark ten feet long was wheeling slowly to face him. The shark had a broad head and a wide mouth filled with ragged teeth. The mouth opened and closed slowly while small eyes glared at Amikuk. The killer was really a coward, but it was a deadly creature, savage when attacking a cripple, and possessed of teeth as sharp and strong as those of the killer whale. The shark wanted to make sure its surprise blow had crippled the otter before closing in for the kill. Its attack had been cautious; it had made sure Amikuk was not a fur seal, and that the otter was asleep.

Amikuk knew he must surface for air even though that meant losing sight of the enemy for a few moments. He twisted his body upward and thrust his head above water. As soon as he had sucked in a deep breath, he called loudly for help. He was surprised because he could not see his par-

*With a frantic effort Amikuk sent his body into
a sharp turn.*

ents or the kelp bed or the rocky reef; all he could
see was waves and sky. He did not wait, but dived
again. Looking at the huge shark was terrifying,
but it was better than not knowing where the killer
was or what it was doing. He went down and again
his efforts drove him in a tight circle.

As he turned he saw the shark. It was still circling, but the circle was getting smaller. Suddenly
the killer swerved away from Amikuk, making a

run which ended in a tight turn. With distance to give it speed and shocking power, the shark could strike a killing blow. It shot forward, straight at Amikuk, its huge mouth gaping open, its little eyes staring straight ahead. With a frantic effort Amikuk thrust outward with his flippers, sending his body into a sharp turn. He felt the fin of the shark slice past him, and a rush of water tossed him aside. But he did not feel a jolting blow. The shark had missed him. When he landed with a splash, he dived. The shark was circling again. It was slow and clumsy but he know it could move fast once it got started. Slowly it circled, planning upon delivering one more crippling blow before using its teeth.

The first wild panic had left Amikuk. He was still alive, and he had dodged the attacker's rush. He knew he must reach the kelp bed, and his fine sense of direction told him where it lay. He started swimming it that direction, watching the shark over his shoulder. The killer had no intention of letting its victim escape. It swerved and moved like a gray-blue shadow, gaining speed rapidly. Amikuk struggled on until the shark was close behind him, before making a frantic turn. Again the shark shot past, and the water it hurled aside sent Amikuk tumbling over and over. For an instant his head was out of the water. He looked for his parents and the kelp bed but could not see them. Snatching a breath, he went down again.

The killer was now convinced the little otter would not fight, and this made it bolder. It made only a short run before turning to strike again. Amikuk ducked wildly as the big mouth snapped shut close to his flippers. The shark did not rush on to make a wide turn as it had done before; it turned fast and was close upon Amikuk when it struck again. Amikuk lashed out with his flippers and shot under the shark. He realized suddenly that the numbness had left his back. His flippers were working the way they should, sending him forward swiftly and in the direction he desired to go. This gave him new confidence, and he darted away in the direction of the kelp bed.

The shark pursued him. Its speed was greater than his, once it got underway. His advantage lay in the lead he could get while the shark was gathering speed. Again he was forced to duck and dive as the shark closed upon him. His training at water tag was serving him well. The ducking and turning enabled him to elude the big mouth and the ragged teeth. Surfacing quickly, he caught a glimpse of the kelp beds through the mist. When he went down, he dived deep. Above him he could see the shark wheeling for another run. He leveled off and moved toward the kelp forest. The killer came down in a steep dive, but Amikuk had flashed into the safety of the ocean jungle before the shark could reach him. He wiggled and twisted until he was deep inside the mass of fronds. Finally he halted and surfaced with his head covered with seaweed. The shark had not followed him, but he was sure it was lying outside the jungle waiting for him.

Amikuk lay perfectly still for a half-hour before venturing to the edge of the kelp bed. When he reached open water, he dived and looked for the shark. He could not see the big body. There were many fishes swimming about but no shark. He waited another half-hour before heading for the reef where he hoped to find his father and mother.

He found them swimming about, anxiously looking for him. They had both sensed trouble and were worried. Amikuk had been missing longer than he had ever stayed away before. He swam to Bobry and huddled close against her. He still needed her and wanted her near when trouble came. She fondled him eagerly and made soft sounds. Kahlan swam around them, lifting his bristling muzzle to look at them, then scanning the water around them. Amikuk stayed by his mother's side for a long time.

11 : MEAT FOR WINTER

It took six days to drive the sea lions to the village. The weather was cold and damp, which made the task easier. Peter used his father's pink parasol to make the lagging bulls hurry along. They were terrified by it and floundered, bellowing wildy, when he thrust it toward them. The smaller, more agile cows and the youngsters took the lead. The big bulls trailed behind and had to rest often. The whole procession strung out over the moss-covered slopes in a long file of plodding beasts.

By the time the procession neared the village, the big bulls were kept moving only because they refused to let the cows go on and leave them. When they halted, they faced the drivers with sullen and surly anger and would not stir until the cows had been driven out of sight. Peter and the men had plently of help long before they reached the village. Old Luca and those men who had brought the bidarkees back to the village had reported, and the people swarmed out to help bring home the winter meat.

Kahgo and Saan were waiting in the village when the herd arrived. There was much shouting and excitement. The village boys looked upon Peter as a grown hunter. They gathered around him and asked many questions.

"Were you not afraid of the sea lions?" one boy asked.

"There is no danger," Peter answered. "Unless a big one wishes to reach the water and you try to stop him."

The boys nodded their heads solemnly. They knew all about a drive, but even so it was hard to believe that the hunters could master such savage beasts. Peter moved away from the boys to help the men drive stakes and string rope for a corral. The sea lions would be held until they could be killed and cut up.

While Peter and the drivers worked, Old Luca and the rest of the village men held a council. They had to discuss the handling of the animals. They owned one rifle and the cartridges for this gun had been counted. There were not enough to kill all of the big bulls. The cows and young animals could be dispatched with a spear or lance, but the hunters knew that if they attacked an old bull with a spear, the big one would smash it to splinters between his powerful jaws. There would be two bulls left after the cartridges had been used. The trader who ran the store did not stock ammunition for the one rifle. It was finally decided that the two bulls left after the cartridges were used up would be headed toward the sea and allowed to escape.

Peter helped his mother dress the cow sea lion that Kahgo speared. Together they skinned the carcass, then she cut off the palms of both fore flippers to be used as soles for boots. She worked swiftly and with a sure knowledge of her job. Each part of the carcass would be stored for use. The stomach would be dried and used as a container for oil, the intestines would be stitched into waterproof garments. Layer after layer of fat was removed to be rendered into oil. The choicest cuts of meat were the hams and loins.

The family would work at least a week getting the meat and the skins cared for. Peter and Kahgo packed the supplies to the hut while Saan worked at the killing ground. The coming winter weather would keep the meat as fresh as any deepfreeze. Peter and his father built a stone-covered pit so that wild animals could not carry the meat away. Kah-go's share was the meat of one large cow and two skins. The skins were carried to the hut where Saan would tan them for selling.

By the time the meat was cared for Peter was very tired of sea lion hunting. He was restless and eager to be off in his kayak fishing and exploring. The big waves offshore seemed to be calling to him. Having spent almost two weeks on land, he was eager to feel his little boat under him. If he had lived in the village, he would have learned to play with the other boys. Living alone with his parents, he had always had to amuse himself, and he had come to love his kayak. It allowed him to adventure far from home. As soon as his last task was finished, he was off, trotting down to the landing with his paddle over his shoulder.

The sea was rough and a challenge to him. For a time, he rode the racing surf in and out between the rocks of Black Reef where he had spent so much time during the summer. He did not expect to find the otter family, but he looked for them anyway. Tiring of surf riding, he headed out to sea. He knew there were islands offshore and decided to locate some of them.

Hours later, Peter sighted the island where Kahlan and his family made their home. It was so barren and devoid of life that he would have passed it by if he had not caught sight of three heads bobbing in the surf near a kelp bed. He worked his way along the rocky shore and moored the kayak back of a rock. From cover, he watched the otters at play. He was sure that they were the friends he had come to know. The youngster was big now and swam as well as his mother and father. Peter watched for an hour before he slipped away unseen. He smiled to himself as he paddled toward the mainland. He had a secret and he would never reveal it to anyone. Old Luca would never know there were three prize pelts so close to the village, and in a place where a club attack on a stormy day would make taking the otters a very easy thing.

That night as he sat beside the iron stove, his mother caught him smiling to himself.

"What are you thinking?" she asked gently.

"It is a secret I will tell to no one," Peter answered, and he continued to smile.

His mother nodded her head gravely. "If it is a good secret you must not tell anyone."

"I will keep it," Peter said. He nodded his head sleepily. Old Luca would never know about the otters. They would be safe on the lee side of the barren island. He got to his feet and pushed the curtain aside. His feather bed was very inviting, and he hurried to get ready to crawl into it.

Amikuk quickly recovered from his encounter with the shark. He did not forget the rows of ragged teeth or the little pig-eyes, and remembering made him watchful, but he wanted to do things by himself, without the eyes of Bobry following every move he made. One day he slipped away and swam along the reef. He stayed close enough to the kelp jungle so that if a shark appeared he would be able to dart to safety.

Nature was flying all of her storm signals, a fitful wind coming in gusts out of the north, a damp pressure in the air, black fog that scudded as it swirled over the white-capped waves. Kahlan and Bobry had read the signals and were waiting for the storm to break, but they meant very little to Amikuk. They made him restless and uneasy but he did not know why. He kept on swimming along the reef, exploring inlets and riding breakers that raced inshore.

He was well out toward the tip of the reef when the storm broke. A great blast of wind filled with heavy sleet swept over him, obliterating everything around him. Huge waves rolled in and crashed upon the unseen rocks close by. Amikuk was lifted high by the first big wave. The sensation of being tossed high into the air did not frighten him; instead it filled him with wild elation. He flipped over and dived down into the trough of the wave and shot through the oncoming wall of the next breaker. It was like tumbling into a deep, green-walled canyon. Stroking strongly, he shot upward to ride the crest of an even higher wave. The sleet tore at him and stung his nose; he was enclosed in a white world that was fast turning grayish black.

But the battering of the wind and the water was beginning to take effect, and Amikuk dived deep and headed back along the reef. The water was shallow, and the currents set up by the turbulent sea were powerful even below the surface where he was swimming. He darted along, ducking and twisting when the sucking currents hurtled him toward the black rocks of the reef. When he surfaced, he was pounded mercilessly by wind and water. He called loudly for his mother, but the wind smothered his voice. And always there was the booming roar of the surf as it smashed upon the rocks. He could challenge the angry sea for a while, but he knew that soon he would tire, and then he would be hurled upon the rocks.

He was not sure of the spot where he had left

Bobry and his father, and he could see nothing but sleet and foaming water. All he could do was to keep on struggling against the storm. He was panting and his flipper muscles were becoming weary. The ragged rocks seemed to be reaching out to pull him to them. Twice he slid between big boulders that leaped into sight only a few feet from his nose, and each time he rode the receding torrent back out to where the next wave caught him up. He lacked the strength and wit Bobry and Kahlan used to master a storm. He had not learned enough.

He struggled weakly as a boiling current caught him. He could not swim against it, and it tossed him swiftly toward shore, lifting him and flinging him far. But when he landed it was not upon the black rocks but upon a churning bed of seaweed. He used the last of his strength to burrow deep down among the weeds. The churning mass protected him from the wind and the sleet. He lay whimpering and panting, afraid to move.

Far down along the reef Bobry and Kahlan braved the storm for hours seeking their son. Kahlan stayed beside Bobry, knowing that if they were separated they might not find each other again until the storm was over. Finally they had to quit the search and seek shelter in a bed of seaweed close to a sand beach, above the wash of the surf.

They buried their heads in heaps of seaweed and waited. Bobry called often but her voice was swallowed by the howling of the wind and the booming of the waves battering nearby rocks.

Amikuk was not inshore far enough to escape the pounding of the gale. The kelp around him twisted and writhed and slapped against his body. He managed to keep his head covered but he could not lie still. He was tossed about like the floats on the kelp. At last the mass where he lay was ripped loose from its mooring and hurled toward the beach. Amikuk was rolled up in a rubbery mass of fronds and tenacles. He had to struggle to keep from being strangled and smothered as the kelp moved toward shallow water swiftly and then changed course and plunged back toward the deep water.

His frantic kicking and clawing finally freed him, and he was able to wiggle free of the mass. The instant he could use his flippers, he struck out for shore, riding a strong current. He found more seaweed and burrowed into it. He kept working his way deeper and deeper into the tangled growth until the pull of the surf lessened and he was able to rest without being battered. Here the seaweed was matted and free from the angry currents. He burrowed down and lay waiting, listening to the storm, raising his own voice every few minutes.

Amikuk was not alone in his struggle against the storm. A half-mile out from the island, a coastwise motor launch was wallowing helplessly. She was a decked boat used for the delivery of light supplies to the trading posts along the coast. Though not designed for heavy cargo, she was a sturdy craft capable of riding out any ordinary storm. But her rudder was smashed and her motor was dead. Six men clung to her deck, seeking shelter in the lee of her forward cabin. None of the crew would stay below, each man strained his ears to catch the first sound of surf booming upon rocks. They were not sure where they were, how near the chain of islands extending out from the Alaskan shore. They knew there were more than the main islands to worry about; there were the many scattered islands shown upon the charts. Only if they did not run aground, did the ship have a chance to survive.

Then the six men heard the booming of surf upon rocks, and they knew the end was near for their ship and perhaps for themselves. Now it was a matter of sheer luck if any of them would live when the ship hit the rocks and broke up. They peered into the wall of swirling sleet and snow, unmindful of its sting. They would have little warning before the crash came. The ship would be on the rocks seconds after the shore loomed out of the storm.

They could judge a little by the sound of the surf crashing over the rocks. The sounds grew louder and the men separated a little, each setting himself for a plunge into the icy water. The small boats were useless; all but one had been smashed. They were rugged men, strong swimmers, but they knew that the odds were against them.

The ship lurched and keeled far over. A shudder passed through her. She had struck a submerged rock. For a few brief moments she held fast; then she lurched forward, listing far to the port.

The men shouted to one another but no one could hear the words, and no one cared about orders or needed any. The captain fought his way to a companionway and lurched into the hold. He did not know why he went except that it was his duty to check damage below decks. He was met by swirling water pouring in through a gaping hole in the port side. He pulled himself back on deck and arrived just as the first seaman went over the rail. He braced himself and waited until the last man had leaped before plunging into the sea himself.

The deserted ship staggered on, settling deeper into the water and listing sharply. Great rocks loomed out of the storm. The ship seemed to hesitate a moment before lifting herself high on a wave and crashing down upon the rocks. The surf buried her in a smother of foaming water. When it receded, she hung upon the rocks, waiting. A returning wall of water smashed over her and she started breaking apart. But she was tough; she had fought the sea for many years. Her builders had put her together with care and knowledge. She stubbornly resisted, but the waves and the black rocks refused to be cheated of their victim. In the end, she broke up, and the angry water claimed her.

Amikuk heard the crash as the ship struck. He was lying close to the rocks where the ship had run aground. He lifted his head and saw nothing but sleet and snow. He knew the strange sound was not made by wind or waves. He had never heard such a sound before. He wanted to get away from the spot, but he dared not leave the sheltered bed of seaweed. As he was staring and listening to the sounds coming from the dying ship, he saw three forms stagger past him, wading waist-deep through the seaweed-choked water. The three upright-walking animals were dragging a fourth between them toward shore. Amikuk ducked his head and buried it deep in seaweed. He was frightened, but there was no way to escape, no place to go.

The storm raged for two days, then broke up as suddenly as it had started. For a time the waves were so wild that Amikuk dared not venture away from the shallows, but at last he worked his way toward open water. He looked for the thing which had made the strange sounds but saw nothing. The waves were still running mountain high, but the air was calm and the sea clear of fog, except for a bank far out at sea. He swam strongly, raising himself high out of the water at intervals to look for his mother and father.

He found them out beyond a kelp bed diving for sea urchins. He suddenly realized he was hungry, but he did not rush to his mother to nurse. Instead, he swam to her side and dived. When he surfaced with food, Bobry swam to his side and nuzzled against him, calling softly to him, petting him. Kahlan moved close, too, and let him know he was glad Amikuk had returned safely.

It was after they had finished their meal that Kahlan discovered the men on the island. They had fashioned a crude shelter out of rocks, and canvas and planks salvaged from the wreck. They had managed to build a fire, and the smoke drifted out over the cove. It was this wood smoke which had alerted Kahlan. He had learned to flee the moment he smelled smoke. Smoke meant the presence of hunters. He sounded the alarm, and this time Bobry did not hesitate. She and Amikuk followed him when he swam away from the island. Again they must seek a new home. Kahlan set his course toward the mainland, and they swam steadily for hours. As day began to fade into night, they sighted a shore. Nearing the shore, they saw a reef and a cove and an expanse of kelp. Bobry quickened her pace, and Amikuk stayed close to her side. They were both hungry and wanted to dive for food. Kahlan hung back long enough to make sure there were no human habitations along the shore and no bidarkees beached near the water.

They moved inside the reef and soon discovered a submerged reef. Happily they started diving for their supper. They finished and feasted long after darkness had settled, and when they had eaten all they wanted, they sought shelter in a kelp bed and slept.

12 : BACK HOME

Quite by accident Kahlan and Bobry had returned to the reef and the cove where Amikuk had been born. They did not recognize it as their old home. It was exactly like a hundred other coves and reefs and kelp beds. There were no landmarks, just the waving kelp and the black rocks rising out of the water. They had always stayed well out away from the shore and the cliffs so that these landmarks meant nothing to them.

Now they had neighbors who had stopped in the cove to spend the winter. Three old bull fur seals had settled in the cove because it was an excellent fishing bank. They were fishermen who knew all of the best fishing banks as far south as the shores of California. They had traveled much in their younger days. As they grew older and heavier, they settled closer to the islands to which they would return in the summer. They paid no attention to the otters, but the otters were curious about the seals.

Amikuk kept a considerable distance between himself and the fishermen at first, but when they ignored him, he swam closer, and soon he was drifting within a hundred feet of them, watching them fish. The bulls were not long away from the island where they spent their summers, each the center of a large band of females. They had fasted during that time, never leaving the small plot of rocky beach which was their harem, and never eating anything at all. They gradually became reduced to lank frames covered with flabby skin. Their bodies were scarred from wounds they had received in battles with other bulls who sought to steal some of the females.

Now they were regaining their strength and building up their bodies. As soon as strength and muscle were rebuilt, they would start adding layers of fat and blubber to their necks and shoulders. This stored food and fuel would be used to carry them through another summer of fasting. Each seal caught and devoured over forty pounds of fish each day.

Amikuk often dived down to watch them as they shot through the water in pursuit of a fish. No cod or halibut or trout could escape them once they gave chase. Several times Amikuk tried to keep up with one of the seals, making it a sort of tag game, but he could not match the speed of the seals. They slipped away from him like flashing shadows.

These seals never played games, all they did was fish and sleep. Every day they hauled themselves out onto a rocky ledge near the center of the reef and slept. Their sleep was restless and filled with spasms and much jerking of flippers. They could, and sometimes did, take naps out in the open water, floating along as easily as the otters, staying half awake and alert to danger from killer whales or hunters.

Bobry and Kahlan soon lost interest in the seals, but Amikuk visited them every day and spent much time staring at them. It was while he was watching them one day that he came to know they were really friends of his, even though they did not know it. He was floating on his back watching a big seal riding the waves and napping. The big fellow had been too lazy to haul himself out onto the rocky ledge. Amikuk was startled by a dark form rising out of the depths toward him. He might not have seen it if he had not had his head turned to watch the seal. It was a toothed shark and it was coming very fast.

Amikuk dived and headed for the kelp bed. It happened that the drowsing seal was between him and safety he sought. Amikuk darted under the seal with the shark in close pursuit. The seal awakened instantly and dived with a powerful thrust of its flippers. Looking back, Amikuk saw that the shark had swerved and was running away with the seal after it. He stopped retreating and turned about to watch.

It was clear the shark was seeking escape, and that it was in a frantic hurry. It swam as fast as it could, but the seal overtook it and shot above it. The shark turned with a frantic lash of its tail. The seal went down in a tight turn and under the shark. Its long tusks ripped at the belly of the killer. Blood stained the water as the seal struck again. In less than half a minute, the eight foot monster was writhing in death agony. The seal swam away without looking back. Within a few minutes, he was busily diving and catching fish.

Amikuk rose to the surface and lifted his head above the water. The seal had joined the other two bulls and they were busily diving and quickly moving about in pursuit of a school of herring. He watched them with new interest. They were fearsome fighters, able to kill a toothed shark. He dived to see what had happened to the shark. It was best to be careful, the killer might still be alive. The shark circled slowly, belly up. Its tail still worked slowly sending the body around in a wide circle. As Amikuk swam closer the shark began to sink. It settled down into the green water, still circling, and disappeared from sight into the black depths. The sight of the huge head and the rows of teeth sent Amikuk darting away. He knew he would always be afraid of killer sharks.

It was Peter who discovered the marooned sailors on the barren island. He set out to visit his otter friends as soon as the storm was over. The blow had not lasted as long as many winter storms, but it had been the wildest he had ever known. While it was at its height, neither he nor his father had been able to leave the hut. Peter wondered how the otters had managed. He knew the barren island offered no protection from the storm. There were no cliffs on it to break the wind.

As he sent his kayak surging toward the rocky shore he was startled to see four men standing on the highest rock on the island. They were waving wildly to him, and as his little craft shot in toward a strip of beach, they came running to the shore. Their faces were gaunt and bearded, and their clothing was torn, but Peter knew they were men off a big ship. They broke into wild laughter as he unlaced the kayak opening and stepped out of the boat. For a moment, he felt like shoving off and paddling away. One of the men held out a hand.

"Boy, are we glad to see you," he said. "Can you bring boats to take us off this rock?"

"I will tell the village men," Peter said. "They will bring the bidar." That was the one large open boat at the village.

"Our ship was wrecked," another man said.

"Could you hurry? We're hungry and nearly frozen," another man said.

"I will go fast," Peter promised. A wrecked ship was always an exciting thing. It meant salvage for the villagers. Cargo from an abandoned ship belonged to any who found it.

The men watched eagerly as he laced himself into his kayak and shoved off. He rowed as fast as he could, but he did take time to look back at the kelp bed on the lee side of the island. He saw no sign of the otters and guessed that they had fled because of the marooned sailors. He did not paddle directly to the village but set his course for his father's hut.

He beached the kayak at the landing and ran up

the path to the hut. He found his mother in the hut and breathlessly told her about the sailors and the wreck.

"Your father is in the village," she said, then added, "Those men must be cold and hungry."

"They looked cold and hungry, but they all laughed when I met them on the shore." Peter frowned.

"They were happy to see you," his mother said as she pushed him toward the door. "You must hurry."

"I will hunt for things from the wreck," he called back to her.

She laughed and closed the door. Peter hurried down to the landing and got into his kayak. He meant to go along when the village men rescued the sailors, and he knew there would be no room for him in the open boat. He did not intend to miss looking for treasure.

The whole village was excited when Peter told them about the shipwreck. All of the men rushed to get into their waterproof clothing. Old Luca picked a crew for the open boat, and the rest of the villagers manned their bidarkees. As they prepared to shove off and follow Peter, Old Luca asked for the tenth time, "Did you see wreckage on the shore?"

The other men crowded around eagerly. The children and the women pressed close around Peter.

"I did not see the ship or any cargo," Peter said. "I think it may have struck the rocks across the island from where I landed."

Everyone nodded their heads eagerly. There had to be wreckage and cargo washed ashore.

"There will be cargo," Kahgo said. "There is always much cargo in a ship."

The women and the children started chattering loudly. Old Luca gave the signal for his crew to push the bidar into the water. Kahgo was one of the three men he had selected to man the open boat. The other men were already laced into their bidarkees. Peter scrambled into his kayak and made himself ready. When he shoved off, a shout went up. The kayak shot away, followed by the open boat and flanked by the bidarkees from the village. Within a few minutes, there was not one seaworthy boat left on the beach. The men shouted back and forth as the boats rode the heavy swells.

The weak and shivering seamen were waiting on the beach when the little fleet arrived. They were so happy over their rescue that they did not complain when they learned that the Aleuts had neglected to bring food. Old Luca wanted to wait until he and his crew had joined the other village men in searching for salvage, but the captain of the ship was not willing to do this. He told Old Luca that there was very little salvage aside from timbers and a few pieces of ship gear. The old man had to be content with the prospect of a reward of money from the captain. Disappointedly the four villagers shoved off for the village with the rescued men huddled in the bottom of the bidar.

The villagers knew that what was cast up by the sea belonged to those who found it, and they searched the entire shore line of the island until they came to the spot where the ship was wrecked. The rocks that the ship had struck were well out from the shore and most of the cargo lay in deep water. There was valuable salvage in the form of planks and boards, and these would be hauled away later. The hunters found a number of cans with the labels washed away containing fruit and tinned meats. They were eagerly gathered up to be opened at home. Peter arrived at the scene of the wreck too late to find any canned goods. He walked along the shore looking for anything that might have been cast up by the waves.

He was sorry he had nothing to take home to his mother. Looking out at the black rocks, he saw the spot where the ship had foundered. A cable and some chains were wrapped around a big rock. He moved down to the water's edge to examine a pile of rocks which the waves were washing. He saw a bundle wedged between two rocks. Following an outgoing wave, he ran to the spot and pulled the bundle from between the rocks. It had been wrapped in heavy paper, but most of the paper had washed away. Peter saw that his prize was a bolt of cloth. It was grimy and water-soaked but that did not hide its bright red color. Eagerly he hugged it to him as he danced up and down. This would make a wonderful gift for his mother.

The canned goods and the bolt of cloth were all that the villagers found. Some of the canned food had been eaten by the shipwrecked men, but what there was would be a treat for the lucky men and boys who found it. Canned fruit was highly prized.

Peter left the village fleet and headed straight toward home to give his prize to his mother. He sent the kayak skimming along at as fast a pace as he could manage. He beached the boat and dashed to the hut.

His mother was delighted with the cloth. There was enough so that she could use some of it for trading. When they unrolled a few yards, they found that the water had not harmed the woolen fabric.

"I will make clothing for you and for Kahgo and for myself," she said.

Kahgo arrived late from the village. He and the bidar crew had returned to the island after bringing the shipwrecked men safely to the village to be cared for by the women. They had found nothing, but each had received some silver from the captain. Kahgo was delighted with the bolt of red cloth, and they spent some time talking about what Saan would make out of it. There would be shirts for the men and a dress for Saan, possibly two coats to be worn when there was a festival in the village.

The villagers supplied the shipwrecked men with a boat which would carry them to a village where trading vessels stopped. The captain gave Old Luca what silver he had on his person, and Old Luca distributed it among the village men. Because of the prize Peter had found, Kahgo did not get any of the silver.

13 : HUMPBACKS

Amikuk finally learned to do cartwheels. He had often watched his father admiringly as Kahlan spun over and over across the cove. He had tried many times to place his paws on the knees of his hind flippers and bend his body into a ball which could be propelled across the water like a pinwheel. At last he had succeeded, and he kept on spinning over the waves until he was dizzy. He whizzed past one of the big seals, and the fisherman raised his head high out of the water to stare at the little otter. It was the first time the old bull had paid any attention to Amikuk.

Their old home was more sheltered than the island had been. Jutting headlands and high cliffs shielded it from the savage winds when the gales swept in from the north. The water was rough and choppy and white-capped most of the time, but the family was never pounded and beaten as they had been while living near the island.

During that winter, Amikuk learned about the dwellers of the deep and those that kept to the shallows, and he met other wanderers besides the three old seals. A school of humpback whales visited the cove. Amikuk awakened one morning to find the cove and his favorite diving ground filled with broad glistening gray-black backs. He raised his head high above the kelp bed, and after one look he dived and rushed to find his mother. The monsters looked fearsome as they lazily rose and sank. Each time a big fellow surfaced, he blew with a sonorous whistling sound. One of the whales surfaced close to the kelp bed where Amikuk was searching for his mother. He ducked and slid down among the fronds.

He expected to find Bobry and Kahlan hiding in the kelp bed, but they were not there. Finally he raised himself and looked out toward deep water. He was startled to see them swimming out over deep water with whales all around them. In order to reach his mother he would have to swim close to at least a dozen of the giants. He hesitated a long time before edging away from the kelp bed. He watched the humpback nearest him until the whale sank slowly out of sight. Then he darted forward

One of the whales sur-faced close to where Amikuk was searching for his mother.

and swam swiftly toward his mother. He changed course quickly as a gray-black back arose in his path. Ducking and diving frantically, he finally reached his mother's side. She was floating placidly on her back eating a sea urchin. Kahlan surfaced and broke open a shell. Neither of them seemed worried, though they were watchful lest a surfacing whale give them a spill.

The humpbacks had little to fear unless they met a pack of killer whales. The humpbacks were not prized by whalers because they were lean fighting creatures, who, when struck with a harpoon, would run like an express train for fifty miles or more, dragging a boat and crew after them, or they would go down in the shoals and roll the iron free or break off the shaft on submerged rocks.

Amikuk pressed against his mother's side nervously. He watched the flocks of whalebirds rising and alighting upon the watery area where the whales were feeding. The whalebirds stayed with the school of humpbacks wherever they went. Hunger finally overcame his nervousness, and he dived down to the underwater reef where he secured a sea urchin. Surfacing, he broke it open and started eating, but he kept an eye on the monsters. They went on feeding and none of them paid any attention to the family of otters. The prey they sought, called "brit," was small, so small Amikuk had never noticed them even though there were millions of the minute creatures. The whales scooped them up and strained the water from them before swallowing them.

Finally the whales moved out of the cove to deeper water. There they stopped feeding and started sporting. They rushed about at great speed churning the water into foaming spray, leaping high above the waves and smashing the water with their massive flukes. A number of them shot into the air and stood for a few seconds on their tails before plunging back into the ocean. Amikuk watched the antics of the whales with much interest.

The sport was broken up suddenly by the approach of a pack of killer whales. The moment the humpbacks sighted the tall fins of the killers, they dived and scattered in wild flight, heading down along the coast. Kahlan saw the black fins and sounded an alarm. Amikuk and Bobry darted away after him to the safety of the kelp bed. From inside the jungle, they watched the wolves of the sea attack a big whale.

The humpback was a giant compared to the killer whales, but it was no match for their savage fury. Its only hope lay in outrunning the killers, and this it tried to do. But the wolves of the sea were faster than the bulky whale. They overtook it and closed in on each side and under it. One fastened itself to the whale close to its head while another struck on the other side. Their long teeth sank deep and they hung on. The whale leaped high out of the water and shook them from it. But when it sank back, the two killers struck again, ripping and tearing and holding on. Others struck from below and from behind.

The humpback fought gamely. His powerful tail smashed one of the killers and left it floating belly up and helpless, but the others came on relentlessly. The big whale turned and plunged into shoal water near the point of the reef. Unless he could free himself of the slashing teeth, he would die. He was fighting blindly, paying no attention to where he was going. He plunged ahead, beating the water to bloody foam, lunging and shaking himself, leaving a crimson wake behind him. Straight past the point of the reef and on toward the rocky shore the humpback charged. He rode a big wave that carried him over the first ragged rocks. His speed and weight sent him high up on the rocks above the wash of the waves where he lay lashing and twisting. Two of the black killers still clung to his head. The rest of the pack ranged close to the rocks, rising out of the water to stare at the beached monster they had hoped to feed upon.

One of the beached killers loosened his hold and flopped down over the rocks into the water. The other hung on for a time, and when he did loosen his grip, he found himself trapped behind a rock. Side by side the victim and the killer floundered helplessly. Both were air-breathing animals, but neither could survive out of the water.

The battle greatly excited the otters and frightened them. They moved deeper into the kelp bed until a high cliff hid the scene of the struggle from their sight. Kahlan would not let them leave the protection of the kelp for a long time.

Peter had discovered that his friends the otters had returned to the reef. On his way to pay them a visit, he found the beached whales. It was a sight that made him stop and stare. There was no prize the ocean could give to a village as fine as the capture of a whale. Nothing fit to eat was so highly prized. Peter could hardly believe his eyes. Two whales, a small black one and a giant humpback. He could see that they were only recently beached; their bodies were still damp and glistening, and there was no taint upon the wind blowing up from the beach. He forgot about the otters and raced away to tell his father and mother.

In his whole life Peter had seen only one whale beached near the village. The men hunted whales in their bidarkees and harpooned many of the younger ones, but they had to trust to luck to secure a prize. If their crude harpoon killed a whale, and then if the winds were right and the whale floated ashore, the Aleuts secured the meat. This did not happen often. But now a miracle had happened; there was a huge whale beached and waiting.

Peter was so out of breath, he could hardly talk when he entered the hut. Kahgo and Saan were patient, but when he blurted out the news, Kahgo shook his head.

"You dream," he said. "It cannot be."

"Come!" Peter shouted. "I will show you the whale!"

The news was so exciting that Saan ran along with Peter and his father. They clambered up on a cliff, and Peter pointed toward the beach below. The two whales lay on the rocks just as Peter had said. For a long moment neither Kahgo nor Saan could speak a word. Finally Kahgo found his voice.

"I will run to the village!" he shouted. Turning he raced away before Peter and his mother could move.

"We must get baskets and knives," Saan said, and she started running back toward the hut. Peter ran after her trying to decide whether to help her or to hurry on to the village where he knew there would be great excitement. He finally decided that he had better help her. They were both panting and had to sit down and catch their breath when they reached the hut.

"There will be a great feast," Saan said happily.

"We can never eat so much meat," Peter said. "The whale is bigger than the whole village."

The excitement in the village over the news Kahgo brought was greater than that caused by the discovery of the wrecked ship. Within a half-hour the village was deserted. The old men and women hobbled along, and mothers carried their babies on their backs. Everyone had a knife and a basket. As usual Old Luca took charge. He was the hunter whose harpoon head had killed the last whale taken by the villagers. Such a man was an object of the highest respect among his fellow hunters.

The villagers clambered down over the rocks to the beach. There was much laughing and shouting as they swarmed around the whale. Peter and Saan were already there, and she was cutting slices of blubber with a long knife. For a few minutes the villagers stood and admired the whale. They ignored the black one. Beside the humpback, it was just another fish. Kahgo broke the silence.

"It is not so fine a whale as the one you killed." He spoke out of respect for Old Luca.

Old Luca nodded and squinted his eyes. Then he turned to Peter. "You will be a great hunter," he said. "You found this whale."

Peter shuffled his feet and wished he were not standing where everyone could see him. He was happy and proud, but having everyone looking at him made him want to hide.

"We will make a great feast," Old Luca said as he unsheathed his knife and moved toward the whale. His wife followed him with her willow basket.

There was a great feast in the village, and later there would be many skins of oil hung outside the huts, and stacks of gristle and blubber frozen for winter use. At the feast, Old Luca told tales of the days when the Aleuts spent most of their time hunting whales. The men and boys sat around him listening. Yellow light flickered from many candles and from the few lamps possessed by the villagers. The community house was warmed by several stoves. Tonight no one thought of saving fuel.

Old Luca showed the boys how the harpoon head was made by lashing a socket of walrus ivory to a handle five feet long. A tip of notched slate was inserted into the socket. Each hunter put his mark upon his spearhead, which looked like a big arrowhead some twelve inches in length.

When a school of whales was sighted, the hunters would set out in their bidarkees. One man handled the paddle while the other manned the harpoon. Feeding humpbacks ignored the boats so that the paddle man could slide the bidarkee close to the whale the harpooner selected. The harpoon was aimed at a spot just under the stubby dorsal fin of the whale and driven forward with all of the strength the hunter possessed. When the point struck, it pulled free of the socket, and the whale dived with the point buried deep, and close to a vital spot.

As they listened, the men and the boys speared pieces of blubber with their knives and crammed them into their mouths. Old Luca stopped talking long enough to fill his mouth. When he had chewed and swallowed, he went on talking.

"The big one would swim to the open sea and go to sleep for three days. After he had slept three days, his body would float to the surface, and the winds would carry it ashore." He smiled at the boys and speared more blubber. "If Mother Sea wished

172

us to feast, the whale was sent to our beach, and the watchers on the cliffs would see it."

"But that was not often," Old Luca's wife said.

Saan got to her feet, and Kahgo joined her. There were many days of hard work ahead. As much meat as possible had to be cut from the whale and carried to the hut, and there was blubber to be rendered for oil. She wanted to be at work early the next morning. Peter stood up and joined them. He trudged along at his father's side after leaving the community house.

"I have heard my grandfather speak of a village so big its people could eat one whale in day," Kahgo said.

"I do not believe there could be such a village," Saan answered.

Peter smiled to himself. He was more than half asleep, walking along in a dream.

14 : SPRING

Amikuk and his parents remained out beyond the reef. A high wall of cliffs rising out of the sea kept them from discovering the presence of the villagers harvesting whale meat. The booming of the surf smothered the laughing and shouting, and the wind blew steadily inland so that no scent was carried to the otters. The attack of the killer whales upon the humpbacks so upset them that they did not return to their accustomed diving around for some time. It was two weeks before Peter sighted them again.

The winter gales changed to spring gales, but there was little change in their fury. They brought sleet and snow from the north, and churned the bay into towering waves. There was one difference. The birds returned, first the burgomaster gulls seeking nesting places, then the lesser gulls and the ducks, and geese, followed by swirling flocks of little auks. The barren cliffs were alive with them, and the little foxes that had starved and grown gaunt began to get fat again as they feasted on eggs and nesting birds.

The day came when Amikuk was a year old. He still liked to be petted by his mother, but he no longer needed to nurse and he was able to secure his own food. He could swim as fast as she and dive as deep. He was capable of making his own way, but he stayed with Kahlan and Bobry. One day she slipped away, and he could not find her. He swam along the reef and searched the kelp beds without finding a trace of her. When he returned to his father, he could tell that Kahlan was worried. He paddled about restlessly and kept lifting his head above the waves to peer about him. Her absence made Amikuk stay closer to his father's side.

Bobry returned one morning. She came sliding out of the kelp jungle on her back, and swam to where Amikuk and his father were floating. She had her forepaws clasped over her breast. Kahlan moved to meet her, but Amikuk was closer and reached her side first. When he snuggled against her, she called softly to him, but she did not fondle him. He raised his head and saw a small bundle of fur clasped to her breast. The bundle stirred and two big eyes blinked up at Amikuk.

At first he was jealous and angry because his mother was fondling this tiny otter. He swam around her trying to attract her attention. But she was so interested in his baby sister that she did not notice him.

Kahlan was excited and nervous. He stayed by Bobry's side all day. When she placed the baby in a cradle of kelp while she dived for food, he stayed close to it. Amikuk felt lonely and left out of the family circle. And there were other feelings stirring inside him which he did not understand. He felt restless and swam far out into deep water. He stayed away a long time but finally returned hopefully to his mother. She greeted him eagerly enough, but when he tried to get her to play with him she refused. She gave all of her time to the baby, and Kahlan was seldom in the mood for play.

Amikuk was out near the tip of the reef when the three big seals left the cove and headed north toward the Bering Sea. Amikuk swam after them, thinking they would turn back as they always had done before. But they did not turn back and finally he dropped behind. Riding the swells, he watched them until they vanished into the gray mists. They were fat and sleek, ready for a summer on the distant islands of the mist.

A week later a large band of two- and three-year-old seals passed the reef on their way north. They had come over a thousand miles and had almost as many more to swim before they reached their summer home. They were not like the grim old bulls, they frolicked and leaped as they swept into the cove and started fishing for herring. Amikuk swam as close as he dared and lay watching them. They had big appetites and there were several hundred of them. The herring and the cod darted wildly to and fro, but a thousand or more of the fishes found their way into the stomachs of the seals before they stopped fishing. The rocky beach was soon littered with fish heads.

The young seals moved on, and Amikuk became more restless. He was seeking something but did not know what it was. He had ceased being jealous of his little sister, and even played with her when his mother would allow it. And his mother began to pay more attention to him again. He should have been less lonely and restless, but he wasn't. He ventured far from his parents and stayed away for as much as a half day at a time. But his absences did not worry Bobry as they once had, and Kahlan paid no attention to his son's wandering.

It was on a trip beyond the reef one day that he met a family of visiting otters. There was a father and a mother and a daughter, Ato, who was smaller and a month younger than Amikuk. The father and mother were only mildly interested in Amikuk. They were much older than his parents and had long since lost the urge to play and frolic. Amikuk swam to the daughter, and they looked one another over shyly. He thrust his nose forward and she let him touch her. He suddenly felt that he wanted to play, to show this little otter what he could do.

He placed his forepaws on the knees of his flippers and went spinning across the water, turning over many times before he came to rest on his back. Ato watched him, and when he came to rest, she swam to his side. She had never seen her father or mother do pinwheels. She made it clear that she thought Amikuk was a wonderful fellow. She rubbed her head against his side and made eager little sounds. This sent him off in another series of dizzy spins. Ato tried to do a pinwheel, but only succeeded in ducking herself. She came up sputtering loudly and tried again. Amikuk swam around her and watched.

After he had showed her all of the tricks he knew, they played water tag for an hour. They were so interested in their game that they wandered far from her parents. The old otters paid no attention to her and did not call her back. Amikuk showed her the reef and the seaweed beds where the snails and crabs were found. They feasted and played in the tangled mass growing in the shallows.

It was not unusual that the newcomers should enter the cove. It was a natural otter haven, and they soon located the submerged reef where the sea urchins lived. Kahlan and Bobry accepted them though Bobry did not let any of them, even the daughter, get close to her baby. When they approached, she would take her baby in her mouth and swim swiftly away.

Amikuk and his new friend spent all of their time together. They were filled with restless energy which demanded an outlet. They swam far, exploring and frolicking while their parents drowsed lazily close to the kelp beds. They played for hours in the surf that smashed upon the black rocks of the reef. They fished for crabs and limpets in the shallow water. From the first they were inseparable companions, napping side by side, diving and dining together.

Peter discovered them on a rare day when there was a little summer sunshine. He had crept out to his lookout spot to lie in the sun and to watch his friends. He was delighted when he saw the young otters at play directly below him. They were riding a swift current that swept them between two big rocks. Amikuk would dart in with Ato close behind him riding the crest of the wave. When the foaming wave started back, they would flip over and ride it out into the bay again.

After a time Peter saw the two other visiting otters, and then he discovered the baby that Bobry held nestled against her broad breast. He was excited and would like to have told someone about the otters. He knew that the otters were not safe, living so close to the village, but he hoped they would stay because he had come to feel they were his friends. None of the village men fished the cove because there was a fine fishing bank just off the village landing, but some venturing boatman might pass that way and see the otters. Four prime pelts would be a great temptation for the hunters, and he knew how Old Luca felt about otters.

On his way home he decided he might tell his mother about the baby otter, and she would like to hear about the two youngsters who played together. Thinking about them made him feel lonely, and he wished they lived closer to the village so he could have a friend to play with.

He found his mother in the yard plucking auks

that Kahgo had brought in. She smiled up at Peter as he sat down beside her.

"Where have you been?" she asked.

"I was out on the reef," Peter answered.

"That is dangerous," Saan chided.

"I watched a family of otters, but I will never tell anyone but you." Peter reached for a bird and started plucking feathers.

"In the old days, the Russians made slaves of our people and forced them to hunt the otters." Saan laid a plucked bird on a grass mat and reached for another. "Now they slip into the village and pay the men to kill the otters. Then the men have trouble and are taken away." Her fingers moved swiftly as she talked.

"There are six otters and a new baby," Peter said. "If the mother is killed, the baby will die."

"The baby is very small?" Saan asked eagerly.

"I think only a few days old. The mother plays with it the way the village women play with their babies." Peter smiled. "I think she talks to it. And I watched two young otters playing together. I think one day they will be mates."

"You are a good boy, Peter," she said. "You do not think of killing the otters."

"I once did," Peter admitted. "I kept thinking of

the things we could buy with the money." He stirred and turned his head. Kahgo was standing behind him. He did not know how much his father had heard, but Kahgo was frowning.

"Six skins would bring much money," he spoke gruffly.

"And you would be taken away from us," Saan said. Peter looked at his mother. She smiled reassuringly at him.

Kahgo shrugged his shoulders and walked away. Peter let his eyes follow his father. Saan took a half-plucked bird from his hands and started stripping feathers from the plump breast.

"Your father has promised not to hunt otters," she said, and Peter knew that that settled the matter so far as she was concerned. She gathered up the grass mat with the plucked birds on it. "Go to the village and get tea and sugar. We will have a fine dinner tonight."

Peter got to his feet. He did not ask her why she had asked him to do this errand when she knew Kahgo was going to the village. He guessed she had not thought about it until after his father had left.

Peter used his kayak to make the trip to the village. He preferred the boat trip to the path over the cliffs. As he sent the little boat darting along toward the village landing, he saw a motor launch put in from the outer bay. It was a sturdy seagoing craft, and Peter knew it did not belong to the government men who patrolled the coast. Launches like this one came from Siberia or Japan. The sight of it filled Peter with uneasiness. The motor launch was already tied up and its owners gone when Peter arrived at the landing.

Beaching his kayak, he walked up the slope to the trader's cabin. He did not see his father and supposed he had gone to the community house to smoke and talk.

The trader gave him tea and a small bag of sugar. His father's credit at the store allowed them to buy a few luxuries, even though he did live away from the village and did not share the community fur money. Peter tucked the two packages inside his jacket and left the store.

He decided to stop for a few minutes at the community house. He always liked to listen to the stories the men told. He was about to pass a hut when he saw two strangers talking to Old Luca. Peter shrank from walking past the strangers. He stepped back out of sight around the wall of the hut. He heard Old Luca talking to the two men.

"I have talked to the men, and one of them tells me of six otters which can be taken." Old Luca spoke in a low voice.

Peter pressed against the hut wall. He did not feel guilty about spying on Old Luca. He had to know if these men were going to hunt the otters. One of the strangers spoke to Old Luca.

"We will pay you to show us where we can find these otters, that is all you need do."

Old Luca's voice was eager. "I will show you, but the hunters can take them for you. I would lead the hunt."

"We want all of the otters. Your men would not get all of them. We have rifles and we can kill them all," the man said.

Old Luca's voice was angry when he replied. "You will not do so well as the hunters. You may not get even one otter, though you may kill them all."

The man laughed. "Show us the otters and we will take them all."

Peter moved away from the hut. He was careful not to let Old Luca or the strangers see him as he hurried toward the landing. He suspected that his father had told Old Luca about the otters. Telling Old Luca would not be breaking his promise to Saan. He knew that the men could shoot all of the otters, but the bodies would be likely to sink. They might not secure a single pelt even though they killed all of the animals. He was angry because his father had told about the otters. He did not know where to find the government men who protected the otters, and they might not visit the village for weeks. Otters were rare. The men had a great deal of coastline to patrol, and the village was so small they seldom stopped there.

He launched the kayak and got in. After lacing the opening, he paddled away. As he sent the kayak homeward he kept trying to think of a way to save his friends.

15 : THE ATTACK

Amikuk and Ato were enjoying the day. It was blustery, and the gusts of wind piled the surf high on the reef. It was an especially proud day for the smaller one. She had finally mastered the art of doing pinwheels. After her first successful spin, she lifted herself out of the water to see if Amikuk was watching. He spun toward her and righted himself at her side, splashing water over her with his flippers. She darted away and he gave chase.

They went around and around, darting through the waves, leaping and diving, shooting along on their backs with their faces to the scudding clouds above. They darted along the kelp bed where their parents were lazily floating and dreaming. Only Bobry was awake. She was washing the baby, and making a game of it which little sister enjoyed very much. Amikuk and Ato paused to watch and to catch their breath.

Bobry soaped the baby with kelp, lathering every inch of her tiny body; then she rinsed the baby by dipping it into the water. When it cried out, she snuggled it to her breast and crooned softly to it. Amikuk was rested and wanted to be off, but Ato lingered to watch the baby. She stayed until the baby's big eyes closed in sleep; then she darted away with Amikuk beside her.

They both felt hungry and had to decide whether to fish the shallow water or to move out into deep water where they could dive for sea urchins. Amikuk wanted to swim out and dive, but Ato decided she wanted limpets and snails and crabmeat. She had learned that he would always give in and do what she wanted to do, so she swam lazily toward the weed-choked shore. Amikuk made a show of ignoring her and going his own way, but he did not keep it up very long. When she was a hundred yards from him, he turned and swam swiftly after her. She pretended she did not know he was following her, and moved in among the weeds without turning her head. Amikuk poked his muzzle against her and made her take notice of him.

For a half-hour they were very busy eating. Finding choice mussels was no problem. The shallow water teemed with marine life, and they had their choice of a large variety of good things to eat. They ate a little seaweed, having discovered a plant they liked, but they were not vegetarians and ate sparingly of the greens.

Kahlan and Bobry had moved out to deep water to dive for sea urchins. Their new friends had joined them and they were all busily diving and feasting. Bobry had fastened the baby to a kelp frond, and it was sleeping soundly. Several gulls swooped down and floated close to the feeding otters hoping for a chance to snatch a few bits of meat. Kahlan splashed water at them, and they screamed hoarsely as they flapped aside.

Amikuk and Ato were floating at the edge of the seaweed too lazy to swim out and join their parents. The smaller one closed her eyes and dozed, but Amikuk stayed awake, watching the cove and the reef. He liked to watch while she napped, and act as though he was protecting her from danger just as his father watched while his mother slept.

He saw the boat before the old otters were aware of it. It darted around the tip of the reef and swept into the cove. Amikuk sounded an alarm much as he had heard Kahlan cry danger. His cry of warning roused Ato. Her head lifted above the water as she stared at the oncoming boat. She had not learned as much about hunters as Amikuk had, and she was more bewildered than frightened. Amikuk crowded close to her and pulled her down into the water where he tried to get her to hide her head under a mass of seaweed. But she was interested and curious. She wanted a better look at the strange creature which was bearing down upon the four old otters. She shook herself free of his paws and lifted herself out of the water for a better look. Amikuk was frantic because she was exposing more than half of her body.

Out in the cove, Kahlan had sounded the alarm, and the four otters dived deep. Bobry headed straight for the kelp bed where she had left her baby. Kahlan followed her, but the other pair separated and headed for open water. Bobry reached the baby without surfacing, but she knew that once she had taken it in her mouth she would not dare to dive. Kahlan had surfaced beside her and was trying to get her to swim with him toward the open sea and a black fog bank which lay offshore less than a mile away. After a moment or two of hesitation, she swam with him, the baby in her mouth. She knew he would not desert her, but she was filled with fright because she must stay on the surface.

The boat swerved and shot toward them. A long paddle smashed down upon the water and a wild shout rang out. Desperately the two otters strained in an effort to gain more speed, but the boat bore down upon them and the paddle smashed upon the water close to Kahlan's head. Bobry would not dive, and Kahlan would not leave her side. They looked up at the hunter in the boat fearfully, and when he shouted at them, they put on an added burst of speed.

The hunter in the boat kept beating the water and shouting, but none of the blows struck Bobry or Kahlan. Peter kept the kayak close to the otters, trying to make his attack look like a real hunt. It was real so far as the otters knew and they were filled with wild fear. He hated to frighten them and he would have liked to get a closer look at the baby, but there was no time to waste. He knew that the powerboat was at that moment approaching the reef. He hoped there would be time enough to do what he planned. He was sure the men with the rifles would moor their boat and shoot from the reef. That was the way otters were killed when a rifle was used. They would trust to the surf to deliver the bodies to them, and they would depend upon the booming of the waves to deaden the sound

A paddle smashed the water close to Ami-kuk's head.

of their guns. He could not be sure they were not at that moment climbing over the rocks. Their power-boat was fast, much faster than the kayak. Turning away from Kahlan and Bobry, he sent the kayak darting back into the cove.

In the seaweed, Amikuk was still trying desper-ately to get Ato to hide, but she kept her head high above water and stared in wonder at the kayak. Out in the water beyond the reef, her parents were div-ing deep and swimming as far as they could without surfacing. They would soon reach the haven offered by the fog bank.

Amikuk knew Ato had been seen. He tried to get her to leave the seaweed and dive with him. She stared at the kayak bearing down upon them and began to feel fear and panic. When Amikuk darted out of the seaweed and dived, she followed him. For once she was willing to let him take the lead.

They surfaced well out in the cove and a back-ward look showed them that the kayak was follow-ing them. A paddle smashed the water close to Amikuk's head, and a wild shout rang in his ears. There was an angry slap close to his muzzle and water sprayed over him. Amikuk did not know the sound a bullet made when it hit water. What made him and Ato dive was the shouting creature in the kayak. Ato went down beside him and swam strongly, but she was forced to surface sooner than he. When she curved upward, he followed her.

They had barely surfaced when the same vicious slap lifted water between them. This time Amikuk heard a hissing whine just before the water lifted. Gasping only a little air, they went down again and swam toward open water. When they surfaced again they did not hear the slapping sounds, and they were able to breathe deeply. They saw the kayak moving away from them toward the tip of the reef. Back on the rocky reef, they could see two men silhouetted against the gray sky. They dived again, and this time they were clear of the cove when they surfaced.

Instinctively Amikuk headed for the fog bank. He did not stop swimming until they were hidden in the black wall of mist. Once inside the blanket of fog, they slackened their pace, but they did not stop swimming. Amikuk remembered his mother, but he did not call for her. He had not cried out once while they were escaping; he had been on his own, and his only thoughts had been for the safety of Ato. Instincts which had saved the few otters still living along the coast told him that he must keep moving, that he and the smaller one must find a new home.

He did not search for his mother and father, and Ato was satisfied to have him to take the place of her parents. Amikuk headed west, and as they swam steadily forward, the distance between them and his parents widened into miles. Kahlan and Bobry had set their faces east while Ato's mother and father were heading out to sea.

Back on the shore, the two hunters angrily watched a boy in a kayak. He was paddling his small craft away from the reef as fast as he could send it over the water.

"Imagine that Aleut kid trying to kill otters by hitting them over the head with an oar," one of the hunters said.

"The little fool spoiled our hunt. We'd have made a big haul," his companion answered.

"Think they'll come back?" the man asked.

His companion shook his head. "They'll travel a long way before they stop. Six otters, that's more than anyone has seen together in years."

In his kayak, Peter started singing a song his mother had taught him. It was a song about a brave hunter who feared no beast on land or at sea. Then he stopped singing and started laughing. He was thinking about the hunters with their rifles. He hoped they had not gotten a good look at him. They might return to the village and tell Old Luca. But that did not matter. He would face Old Luca. He had saved his friends and he was proud of what he had done.

16 : HOUSEKEEPING

Long after fear had left him, Amikuk kept on moving westward along the chain of islands. He set an easy pace so as not to tire Ato. At least two more years would pass before he was fully grown, but at the age of a year and a few months, it was time for him to be thinking of taking a mate. So far he and Ato had merely been friends and pals, playing and hunting together, but now a different feeling was stirring within them both. Amikuk felt that she was his responsibility. He must protect her and care for her.

Their first stop was close to a kelp bed. They did stop for rest but because Amikuk sighted the black fins of a pack of killer whales on the prowl. He sounded a warning and waited until she had dived before joining her. This time Ato kept her head down. She knew about killer whales. When they surfaced, they swam with just their noses and eyes out of water. A wave lifted them, and they saw the tall black fins cutting the water at terrific speed. The killers were circling, searching every foot of the water they passed through. Their ugly heads were lifted, and their small eyes looked for seal or otter or whale, any living thing big enough to make a meal. Amikuk and Ato dived and swam swiftly toward the kelp bed he had sighted. When they surfaced again, they could not see the tall fins.

Amikuk and Ato were ravenously hungry. They had traveled a great distance without stopping to seek food. They wasted no time in seeking a submerged reef where they could find sea urchins. Amikuk kept a watchful eye on the surrounding water and the fog bank where the black fins had vanished. He dived deep but could not find bottom. The little one dived with him, but gave up after the first attempt. He tried several places but found no reef. Amikuk gave up trying to locate a feeding ground. He was not yet wise about such things. They swam into shallow water and started feeding upon snails and crustaceans. They found a variety of things to eat and feasted for an hour, eating lazily and resting between courses as soon as the edge was off their hunger.

Amikuk knew this was only a temporary stopping

place. The kelp bed lay close to shore and deep water hid the beds where the sea urchins grew. He knew that their most deadly enemy—man—lived on the mainland and hunted along the shore. He looked out over the wild desolation of water and felt that their safety lay far away from the mainland. Like Kahlan, he was thinking of an island with reefs and kelp beds, a desolate island with no man living on it. It was a quest he would make and would keep on making until he found such a place.

Ato was a bit uneasy about heading out into the vast and turbulent ocean again, but she followed Amikuk with only a few whimperings. He swam on until the mainland had faded from sight and there were only the mountainous waves and the gray sky around and over them. But they were not alone in the vastness; gulls swept along overhead, carried by a roaring wind. Their harsh cries were constantly heard. Amikuk was watchful, his eyes sweeping the waters around them. To be sighted by killer whales so far from a kelp bed would mean death.

By the evening of the second day, they stopped to fish. They still had not seen an island or a kelp bed, but Amikuk was sure he would find one. He was not disturbed, except for the hunger gnawing inside him. They could not dive for sea urchins, and there was no shallow water where they could easily find food. They swam underwater, seeking small fish. They worked hard for an hour or more. They succeeded in catching a few, but they lacked the skill of seals and were still hungry when they stopped fishing.

Ato was beginning to show signs of weakening. Although she still trusted Amikuk, she kept looking toward the fog banks beyond which lay the mainland. She stayed close beside him, but he was aware that she might decide to strike out alone if he did not soon discover an island. He coaxed her with eager calls, and they pushed on through the night and the next day.

Toward evening of the third day, they were met by gray banks of fog; it swirled over them on a gale that lashed the ocean into white-crested waves. They had not eaten during the day, and they were both weak from hunger. Ato dropped behind and started diving for sardines and tomcod. Amikuk turned slowly and lifted himself out of the water. He peered about anxiously and called to Ato. For the first time since he had struck out into the vast world of water and sky, he began to worry. He was not so sure of himself and that made him afraid.

Ato gave him a brief look before diving. She did not answer his calls. He paddled in a circle and waited for her to surface. As he floated, he listened intently. Her head appeared, and she stared at him dejectedly. She had not been able to catch a fish. She was tired and lacked the speed to capture the darting sardines.

Amikuk suddenly raised himself out of the water and called excitedly to her. His sharp ears had caught the boom of surf breaking over shore rocks. He was certain that his island lay hidden in the mists ahead. He called again, and started swimming. She hestitated but finally followed him reluctantly.

When she heard the surf, she quickened her pace and they darted forward, diving through the waves, their weariness forgotten. They came to the kelp beds before they saw the shore and followed the waving mass until they came to shallow water where seaweed grew profusely. The fog was so black and heavy that they could see only a few big rocks rising above the water, but Amikuk was sure this was an island, his island.

They busied themselves gathering food and stuffed their stomachs until they could eat no more. Then they lay close together with the swell lifting

Amikuk and Ato were sure this was an island, their island.

them and rocking them. They were snug inside the mass of seaweed away from the pounding waves. Very soon they were asleep, and they did not awaken for a long time.

When they woke up, they found that the fog had lifted. As he had expected, Amikuk saw an island. It was no more than the top of a mountain rising above the water, a craggy, barren pile of rock, but there was a ragged reef, and at low tide there would be a small stretch of beach. On the lee side of the reef lay the kelp beds.

Small as the island was, it had its quota of birds, and a lone bull sea lion had found a home on a ledge. The old fellow was recovering from wounds suffered in a fight with another bull. He was ancient, and his days were numbered. The island had attracted him as he floated aimlessly out to sea. Had he missed it, he would have kept on swimming until his body sank into the depths. He was no threat to the young otters, but they did not venture near his ledge.

Here on the lee side of the island, they mated; it was unlikely now that they would ever be separated except by disaster or death. They played games and spent hours drowsing. Amikuk explored and discovered a submerged reef which teemed with sea-urchins. They seldom remembered their parents, but they did not forget what they had been taught. The days slipped by, and one stormy day the birds started leaving the cliffs, heading south for the winter. Soon the only life on the island was the old sea lion. They settled happily to face the storms and the cold.

In the spring Ato would cuddle a baby, and Amikuk would have greater responsibility; but also greater joy. The savage gales did not worry them at all. They snuggled deep into the seaweed, secure from their enemies until each storm broke.

The long nights and the short days came and went, bringing nothing but peace to the wanderers.

ABOUT THE AUTHOR

RUTHERFORD G. MONTGOMERY has spent a lifetime observing and studying the animals which are his favorite subjects. He was born in 1896 in North Dakota, and as a boy ran a trap line. He wandered all over the Northwest and the West, taught school in Colorado, and served six years as a judge of a court of record in that state before choosing writing as his sole occupation in 1938. Since that time, he has had over fifty books published.

Mr. Montgomery's many books—stories of Western adventure, mystery tales, sea stories, and animal stories like *Amikuk*—have earned him a widespread reputation as a writer for young readers.

Mr. Montgomery, the father of three children, now lives in Los Gatos, California, with his wife Eunice and their younger daughter.